Malice at the Palace

·

Maile Spencer Honolulu Tour Guide Mysteries
·

Kay Hadashi

Malice at the Palace

Malice at the Palace
Maile Spencer Honolulu Tour Guide Mysteries
Kay Hadashi. Copyright 2020. © All Rights Reserved.
Cover art by Kingwood Creations.
ISBN: 9798591086985

This is a work of fiction. Characters, names, places, dialogues, and incidences are used factiously or products of imagination. Any resemblance to actual persons, businesses, events, or locales, unless otherwise denoted as real, is purely incidental. No part of any character should be considered real or reflective of any real person, living or dead. Information related to current events should be considered common knowledge and can easily be found in real life.

Malice at the Palace

Table of Contents

Chapter One 7

Chapter Two 12

Chapter Three 21

Chapter Four 30

Chapter Five 41

Chapter Six 54

Chapter Seven 68

Chapter Eight 77

Chapter Nine 91

Chapter Ten 103

Chapter Eleven 115

Chapter Twelve 128

Chapter Thirteen 144

Chapter Fourteen 156

More from Kay Hadashi 173

Malice at the Palace

Chapter One

It was a morning off, but Maile Spencer wanted to be up early. As a Honolulu tour guide, she had a tour to give later that day with errands to run first. It was so early that Saturday morning, even the neighbors across the hall hadn't begun their morning squabble yet. In fact, the Mendozas hadn't been bickering nearly so much lately, making Maile wonder if they'd worked past their problems. Or had things between them become so bad that they'd given up talking altogether? The answer came when she heard voices out in the hall as she put on her teakettle.

When she peeked out the peephole in her front door, she smiled at what she saw. Rosamie was being fully embraced by her husband, the two of them locked in a kiss. As a recent divorcee, Maile's heart ached for the same thing, a long and passionate kiss. When she saw them finally break, there was a moment of hesitation before Rosamie let her husband's hand go as he left for work. She lingered in the hallway and gave him a wave before the door to the outside world slammed shut behind him. That's when Maile cracked open her door hoping to get a little gossip about their romance.

"Rosamie, care for a cup of tea?"

"Hi Maile! I'd love some. I'll be right over."

"You and the hubby are getting along better lately," Maile said, delivering a mug of breakfast blend tea to her friend.

Rosamie's eyes sparkled. "Feels like our honeymoon all over again."

"Because you're pregnant?"

Rosamie nodded. "Every time he gets me kno...I'm pregnant, I get all dreamy. Someday you'll understand, Maile."

"Someday." After chatting about the baby, Maile decided it was time to bring up what was on her mind. "You said a while back you guys need to find a bigger place to live. Have you found something yet?"

Rosamie bit her lip for a moment. "We have. Since today is the first of the month, I need to give Mrs. Taniguchi one month notice that we're leaving."

That hit Maile pretty hard. "Oh. A month. Where are you moving?"

"We found a little cottage in Kaimuki. Cute place and we had just enough to make a down payment. I didn't tell you?"

"I guess I missed the details," Maile said. "When's moving day?"

"January First. Nice start to the new year." Rosamie finished her tea. "Gonna miss you."

"Me, too. You were my first friend." Maile shrugged. "First away from the hospital, first after leaving my husband. First friend just as a friend."

"You're gonna come visit, right?"

"When I can. I'll be busy after the first of the year."

"You mentioned you're getting busier than ever as a tour guide. Business is that good?"

"Yes. I also heard from my new lawyer that I might have my nursing license back pretty soon."

Rosamie's face brightened. "That's great! More money for a better place to live than this dump. Hey!

Maybe something near us will open up near us and we'll be neighbors again?"

There was a crash of something breaking across the hall in Rosamie's apartment. They both craned their heads to look that way. Only silence came to them.

"Need to go check on that?"

"I'll find it eventually."

"Kaimuki is nice. I have another friend who lives there." Maile took their mugs to the sink to rinse, her latest set of qualms beginning to set in again. "I'd like living there."

When Rosamie's daughter showed up, her normally smooth forehead was furrowed with worry. "Mama?"

"I'm busy, Honey. What broke?"

The girl spoke in a Filipino language that Maile couldn't understand. Whatever had happened wasn't making Rosamie happy.

"Maile, I gotta go check on something. I'll be right back."

Maile waited, washing her few dishes, listening to Rosamie hand out a scolding, and the kids offering alibis in return. All that happened while something was being swept up. It was all quite entertaining, even if she couldn't understand a word of it. When her phone rang, she grabbed it from the table.

"Detective Ota, good morning. You've caught me at a bad time."

"Just calling to make sure you're still coming to the station this morning the way you promised?"

"Of course." There was something she wanted to talk to him about, something personal that she'd heard about him recently, and needed to verify it. Today would be a good day for it. "Have you ever known me not to keep my promise to you?"

"No, but there's always the first time."

"If I ever break my promise to you, you can lock me in a cell with my friends. Maybe you can give me a hint as to what your little meeting is about?"

"Trust me, it's important. How are you getting here?"

"Taking the bus, why?"

"Car still on the blink?"

"According to a friend, it might be time for the junk yard. Why is that so important?" she asked.

"Do me a favor and take a different bus than usual."

Maile wondered what was going on. "Not much choice on how to get there from where I live."

"Take a bus from a different stop than your usual. Maybe go a couple blocks down the street and catch it there."

"How do you know where I catch the bus?"

"It's a bus line along a major thoroughfare across the city. I've spotted you at the stop near your building often enough to know your routine. When will you be here?"

"A couple hours. But I have one or two things to talk to you about, also."

Rosamie came back with her broom and dustpan still in her hands. "Maile, ha! I have big trouble over there right now. Can we talk again later?"

"Okay with me. I have some errands to do anyway before my tour this afternoon."

Rosamie's lecture to her children about something continued after she slammed her door shut at home.

Malice at the Palace

Whatever had been broken, Maile was glad for it. She had a busy morning, and didn't want to think of losing her friend so soon.

"I might be leaving pretty soon, too," she muttered, climbing in the shower, which was, as always, cold. After, Maile dressed in a white blouse and plaid pleated skirt for her tour at the Iolani Palace later that afternoon, about all she had that was clean and pressed. The last thing she put on was a little silk kerchief tied snug to her neck. "Time for a trip to Mom's house for laundry and ironing. How's that for an exciting social life?"

She made a second lap through the kitchen, still looking for something more substantial than tea for breakfast. It wasn't as if her pocketbook was as empty as it usually was, it was a matter of not having enough time lately to shop for groceries. That was a matter of taking a bus to a real supermarket, and then carrying her bags home on the bus again. As it was, her kitchen cabinets were used primarily for storing her clothes, and only to a lesser extent, food. The money she was earning that day would go a long way to filling them. If she bargain shopped, she might be able to help pay a couple of her mother's bills, too. Her brother was on his own, though, now that his college tuition had somehow been paid, enough to hold him for the next few months. Once the kitchen was clean and her small convenience apartment was tidy, Maile left her daily problems behind as she started that day's adventure.

Chapter Two

If Maile worked it right, she could meet with Detective Ota and still have plenty of time for lunch before her afternoon tour. As it was, she was getting to the police station an hour earlier than what she'd told him.

"You look nice today, Ms. Spencer."

"Thanks. I have a tour later. I actually ironed this outfit for a change."

"Not your outfit. Every time I see you, you look fitter. Stronger somehow. Been going to the gym?"

"Maile's Home Gym. I do sets of pushups and situps to wake myself up in the morning, and before I go to bed."

He looked up at her over his half-glasses. "For?"

There was an answer but she wasn't sharing it. For as well as Ota knew Maile's personal business, some things needed to remain private. She shrugged. "Just getting a little stronger."

"Does it have something to do with those abrasions on your elbows?"

Maile tugged her long sleeves down. "Maybe."

"Fall while you were running?"

"In a way," she said evasively.

"Not getting pushed around by a man, are you?"

Maile chuckled. "Is that what you're worried about? Because don't. Nobody's pushing me around without my permission."

"What's that mean?" Ota asked.

"Along with my running, I've taken up obstacle coursing classes. The coach is a retired military drill instructor, and he does a lot of impressive encouragement, but he doesn't force anyone to do anything that's not safe. Somewhat safe, anyway."

Ota went back to sorting through forms. "I've heard about that. Sounds like fun."

"Mostly. Good workout."

"And you're doing that for?" he asked. "Are there competitions?"

Maile smiled. "Maybe in a few weeks."

"You're being especially evasive today."

"I've learned to be when dealing with the police. What did you want to talk to me about? Because you're calling me Ms. Spencer instead of my first name. That usually means something official is about to happen to me, whether I want it or not."

Detective Ota pushed his reading glasses up his nose and shuffled more papers. "There's been a development with your friend, Prince Aziz."

"Not my friend," she hissed. "I wish you'd stop calling him that."

"Whatever he is, there's news."

"He's finally going to prison where he belongs?"

"Not hardly. Remember I told you he'd been released from custody?"

"Yes. So?"

"There's an on-going inter-agency task force stakeout managed by the FBI, and manned by the US Marshals. They've been watching Aziz's movements and activities since he was released a while back. They found an acceleration of activity in the last few days, and asked me to join them over the weekend."

"What're you getting at?" she asked. "Has he done something to more women?"

"Not that we're aware of. The task force has been more concerned with elopement than anything else."

"They think he's going to skip town? Honestly, I'm surprised he hasn't already. But what does this have to do with me?"

"I'm getting to that. A young man from Khashraq, his home country, arrived a week ago. He's very nearly the same size in build, color, and height. He even wears the same style of glasses the way your friend does."

He pushed a color print of the newly arrived Aziz family member to Maile. It looked like an official portrait of some sort.

"Who is he?" Maile asked. She looked closely at the face, a good double for the Prince, almost a doppelganger. Same dark skin, same dark eyes, same large pores on his nose, same white headdress secured to his head with an ornate cord.

"Another Aziz. The Bureau is trying to determine if he's a brother or cousin of some sort. He also flew in on a private Gulfstream, owned by the Aziz family."

"Why do I care about him?" she asked.

"Wait." He handed over another picture. This one looked as though it had been taken by a zoom lens, a candid shot of the young man outside in ordinary Western-style clothes. In this one, the young man had a nearly shorn head, something different from what the Prince kept, that of a bushy but primped style. Other than that, Maile would've guessed it was the Prince.

Malice at the Palace

Maile still didn't know how she was involved. "So, he's going to pull a switch? Pretend he's this other guy and leave on his private jet? If that's the case, let him. Personally, I'm tired of hearing about the guy."

"Your wish has come true, Ms. Spencer. Late last night, he did exactly what you said, pretended to be the other Aziz and left on that plane. He showed proper credentials to TSA, did everything one needs to do. But it was the wrong Aziz, the one we've been watching, that got away."

"How can you be certain?"

"Bureau agents have collected trash and other items of interest, including hair that looks suspiciously like the Prince's. Then they ran fingerprints, and discovered they're from the other Aziz. Prints from the real Aziz are nowhere to be found in or near the place he's been staying. And yes, they've already used Egyptian blue powder to double check for latent prints. The feds are pulling out all stops on this, funding not an issue. They want the Prince behind bars as much as you do. And me."

"No, Detective, not as much as I do. Where is he now?" Maile asked.

"His Gulfstream left Honolulu just before dawn this morning."

"So, that's it, then? He just left and there's nothing anyone can do about it?"

"Sorry. He played us for suckers. And when I say us, I mean the Bureau, the US Marshals, and TSA. He made all of us look like fools."

"Me, too."

"How so?" Ota asked.

"How many times have I been locked in your cellblock because of that guy? Twice? Three times?" Maile crossed her legs and bounced a foot. "Good riddance, if you ask me. Let Los Angeles deal with him for a while."

"Why there?"

"That's where he was originally going next, right?" Maile asked. "Surely you remember the first time you arrested me when he tried to proposition me?"

"The flight plan that was reported to the FAA indicates the plane is headed to Singapore. The last I heard from Honolulu International Airport tower is the flight is maintaining that course and direction." Ota looked at his watch. "He's probably halfway there by now."

"I don't know how these things work, but has somebody here told anyone in Singapore that bad news is headed their way in the form of a creepy Middle Eastern prince?"

"Beyond my pay grade."

"Do you suppose your friends in the federal government have told anyone?" she asked.

"They're as much my friends as the Prince is yours. To answer your question, maybe, maybe not. They're probably glad to be rid of him, also."

"What about the fake Aziz? Can't someone lean on him a little?" Maile asked. "You guys still say that? Lean on guys?"

"Only in the movies. There's nothing we can do with him. He can go whenever he wants. As far as the federal government is concerned, he's done nothing illegal. Jerk, yes. Illegal, no."

"But he'll have to use the Prince's passport to leave, right?"

"There're a dozen ways around that. He could complain his passport was stolen, or simply have a new passport couriered to him from home. With as much money as they have, and his choice of luxury accommodations in Honolulu, he doesn't have to be in a hurry to leave."

Maile got her things ready to leave. "Well, thanks for telling me."

"Don't forget that other fellow is still here in Honolulu."

"So what do I care about him?"

"He has bodyguards and associates."

"And once again, so?"

"They could be looking for you."

"Me? What'd I do to them? Why should a fake Aziz care about me? The real prince got out of the country. That's all they wanted, right?"

"Except you made trouble for their family, and they might want some retribution."

Maile waved her hands in the air in surrender. "They can get it from somebody else. They probably have far more money than I could ever possibly spend in a lifetime."

"It wouldn't be money they want from you."

"What, then? Kidnap me like their original plan? You're making me feel a little paranoid, Detective Ota."

"Maybe a little well-controlled paranoia might be useful right now. The deal with the Prince's prints on the kahili recently make the Feds think there's a new scheme. They think Aziz is done with abduction for sex slavery, at least with you. Something else might be cooking."

"Yeah, well, they can cook it in Singapore."

"One idea the Feds shared with me is that they might be looking for more than a meal, Ms. Spencer."

Maile got a chill. Strangers on the island were looking for her, they weren't tourists, and they didn't want to be shown around Waikiki. "What am I supposed to do?"

"Lay low. Is there anywhere else besides your apartment or your mother's cottage you can stay for a while?"

"Lay low? My job takes me to some rather prominent sites all over this island. How can I lay low?"

"One thing you can do is not take the Manoa Tours bus. They'll be watching for that as much as watching your home and the office."

"It's how Lopaka gets us around. Not much of a tour guide if I make my guests take the city bus everywhere."

"The company has that other bus. Can you trade tours with the other guide for a while?"

"With Christy?" Maile shook her head. "That's her pet bus. Even though I'm taking out more tours and making more money for the company lately, she's got an iron grip on that better bus."

"Figure something out with her. And like I told you this morning, start changing your city bus routes. Take earlier or later buses and catch them from different stops each day."

"You think they're following me?" she asked.

"We have no idea what they might be up to, if anything. But we can't go with you everywhere you go. You need to be vigilant."

"Now I really am getting paranoid. Anything else?"

"Take a change of clothes with you when going out in public. Change your outfit often, and swap articles of clothing around for different looks. Use different bags, wear hats and sunglasses, even on cloudy days." He scanned her face. "You might want to get rid of the little scarf."

She touched a fingertip to the small silk kerchief she often wore. "This is what my guests look for in crowded places. Sort of my signature look, instead of some flag to wave at them."

"Something as simple as that could help the Aziz clan spot you in a crowd. Can you change the way you wear your hair?"

Maile touched the tidy knot of hair that rested on her shoulder. "No. Not because of them, anyway."

"Whatever you can do to look less like yourself would help."

She got her bag and stood, ready to leave. "I'm not hiding under the kitchen table. I need to earn a living and live my life. Believe it or not, this is what a professional tour guide looks like."

"Your tour today is at the Palace? You seem to take a lot of tours there."

"I'm turning out to be Honolulu's leading expert at making up fanciful stories about the Iolani Palace. I'm becoming famous for it."

"Who's in your group today?"

"A group of teenagers from Australia, New Zealand, one of those places. Word is they travel to historical places a lot. I doubt the Aziz clan will infiltrate their ranks. Do you use that word? Infiltrate?"

"I don't, but the feds do." Detective Ota walked her through the usual corridors to the front entrance of the police station. He held the door open for her. "Be careful out there, Maile."

Maile stepped out. "Yes, I know. The world is a weird place and I'm right in the middle of it."

He joined her out on the sidewalk after making a point of shutting the door behind him. "Before you leave, there's one more thing you need to know."

She sighed when her bus went by, just missing it. "About?"

"We had to issue a permit to a group of Hawaiian secessionist protesters."

"That's not me, Detective," she said. "I have nothing to do with those people. If the federal government were to somehow return Hawaiian lands to Hawaiian hands, okay, fine. I'd accept them. But I'm not going to wave signs around or yell at tourists about it."

"You're onto something about yelling at tourists. The protest takes place today at the Iolani Palace."

"That means…"

"You're walking into a bee hive."

Malice at the Palace

Chapter Three

Maile still had three hours before her tour was to start. Most of it was a historical tour of the Iolani Palace, which started with a quick photo op at the King Kamehameha statue nearby. She caught the next bus that stopped, not caring which route it followed. She gave Ota's warnings some thought, about being careful in public and staying away from the Manoa Tours bus. All she could do was take one day at a time, one tour at a time, one bus ride at a time. That day, she was close enough to the Palace and the statue that she didn't need to go back to Waikiki to meet her tour group. Lopaka could just bring them to her.

She gave him a call. "Brah, change of plans. You need to pick up the group without me today."

"Why? What's wrong? You can't be running late. We still have plenty of time."

She gave the crib notes explanation of what Ota told her about how the Aziz clan might still be looking for her, and possibly watching for their tour van. "I seriously doubt they are, though."

"You never know, Mai. Where do you want to meet?"

"At the statue. I'll wait in front of it."

"Maybe you should wait on the front porch of the Supreme Court building? If those guys really are looking for you, there's no reason for you to stand near the street where they might see you. I need to drop off the group there anyway."

"I don't like hiding."

"It's not hiding. It's being safe, Mai. Do everyone a favor and be careful for a while, at least until Ota or whoever can get rid of those Aziz guys. No reason for you to put yourself at risk."

Maile was already in Chinatown, and decided on lunch there. She made a beeline to a small Vietnamese noodle house she occasionally took tour guests for an authentic Chinatown meal. Instead of the fresh spring rolls she enjoyed, she got a bowl of pho, soft noodles in a heady broth full of vegetables and bean sprouts. Half the pleasure of it was inhaling the steam that rose from the bowl that seemed packed full of vitamins. The long, clunky chopsticks she needed to use were worth the effort, because she always felt as though her energy perked up after the meal.

"No tour group today?" Binh asked. Maybe the young woman wasn't the exact owner of the place, but she ran it with an iron grip. That included the full-service salon next door and a flower shop near Maile's apartment building.

"Not till later at the Iolani Palace."

Binh pulled out a chair and sat at the table. "Never have been there."

"You can join my tour today. No charge."

"Thanks. Maybe another time. I have some billing today. Managing these places would be easier if there wasn't so much paperwork."

"I'd make a mess of billing in no time." Maile thought of the legal trouble her ex-husband was in because his 'creative' bookkeeping habits with the pub he owned before selling it to his brother, which could still bring her some legal trouble. It wasn't worth bringing up then, though. She finished with her soup and got out her wallet.

"You don't have to pay, Maile. Not after what you did for me a while back. You bring a lot of customers here on your tours, and believe it or not, some of them come back a day or two later. I owe you so much. My auntie wants to adopt you."

"I'll take that as a compliment." She looked at her acquaintance's perfect complexion and glossy hair. She was a walking advertisement for the full-service salon next door. Maile wondered if other things went on there other than hair, nails, and facials. "You guys do massage next door, right?"

"Our newest service. Not many takers yet."

"Is it…"

"Legit?" Binh asked. "Yes. We prefer women. One or two of the guys that have been in for massages have misinterpreted the service. We're trying to turn the place into a spa."

"Do you know if they have time for me?"

"You don't seem like the spa type of gal, Maile."

"Usually, I'm not. I've been doing a lot of running for the marathon coming up in a couple of weeks and my legs feel a little tight. Is that something they can work on for me?"

"That big marathon? Isn't that twenty-six miles?"

"Twenty-six and a quarter miles."

"You can run that far in one day?"

"I hope so." Maile chuckled. "I think that last quarter mile will do me in."

"Funny how that works," Binh said. "You have to run twenty-six miles, just so you can run one last quarter mile to finish the race. Why not just run the quarter mile and forget about the rest?"

The last thing Maile needed right then were negative thoughts to enter her mind about the race. There was an ulterior motive in running the race, though, something she was still trying to convince herself was a good idea. "Sorta like climbing a mountain, I guess. Just to know I can."

Binh took Maile by the arm and led her next door. After a quick explanation by Binh to the massage therapist in Vietnamese about what Maile wanted, she was face down on a massage table in a dark room illuminated by only one small lamp and a few candles. She hadn't taken off her clothes, only covered with a heavy sheet. 'Auntie', one of the regular hairstylists, went to work on her lower back.

"You always give massages to fully-clothed people?" she asked the middle-aged woman.

"Yes."

"Do you like doing this?"

"Yes."

"How long have you been giving massages?"

"Yes."

Figuring she was headed into a one-sided conversation, Maile gave up on chitchat. Instead, she followed with her mind what the woman was doing to her rear end. Soon, strong hands found knotted muscles in the back of her thighs, and they were kneaded until they relaxed. Every now and then, Auntie would say something in Vietnamese, and Maile would simply mumble an agreement.

Malice at the Palace

Next came her calves, what Maile really wanted worked on. When she felt a knuckle grind into a rock-hard muscle, her phone chimed with a call. She peeked at the caller, her lawyer, and knew she needed to take it.

"Hello, David," she said, wincing.

"Have a few minutes, Maile? I have some updates to tell you about."

"Good news or bad?"

"Mostly good. Is something going on there? Did I call at a bad time?"

She had to unclamp her teeth. "It's okay. I'm just getting a massage, which is a lot more painful than what I expected."

"It sounded like...never mind."

"Like what?"

"Like I interrupted a nooner."

"I should be so lucky." Maile blushed as what she'd said to something of a romantic interest. David Melendez was a senior partner in Honolulu's biggest, and most expensive, law practice. Single, handsome, well-spoken, large condo in Waikiki, the nephew of an ex-President. What could be better in a man? "What's the good news?"

"First, the sale of Robbie's bar to his brother Thomas wasn't legal."

"So I've heard from Detective Ota. But I had nothing to do with that. You must believe me. I never once looked at his books. If that makes me stupid, okay, I can accept that. But I'm not a crook."

"Relax, Maile. I believe you."

"What about the judge and District Attorney?" she asked. Auntie started massaging the other calf.

"They won't care. You know why?"

Maile winced through more pain. "I can't imagine why."

"The bar wasn't Robbie's to sell."

Maile lifted her head, now trying to ignore the pain. "What? I put every spare dollar I earned into that place and somebody else besides Robbie owned it?"

"Yes, you do. That's why Robbie couldn't sell it to Thomas."

"I own that stupid bar?"

"Surprise!"

Auntie moved to Maile's feet, turning her ankles in circles. At least there shouldn't be pain with the last part of the massage. "I don't understand. How do I own the bar?"

"There were too many inconsistencies with the bar, the tour company, and two brothers selling businesses back and forth. So, I got copies of the paperwork that were filed with the city and county for business licenses and health department inspections. Your name is all over the title for the place, including your signature. You don't remember signing that?"

"I remember signing a bunch of paperwork at the time, including personal checks, but I was never informed it was for ownership. I'm a lot stupider than I thought, signing things without looking at them more closely. Does that mean I'm in trouble because of his bad bookkeeping?"

"Probably not. The DA has said she likely won't press charges against you, as long as you agree to be a witness in court. Her office has already examined all the legal forms, along with the books that Robbie kept, and they have his handwriting. The best thing for you is that nowhere can your handwriting be found, or your signature, related to billing vendors or his bookkeeping. That means a lot to a DA."

"I've learned that lesson. Not much choice. But what am I supposed to do about the bar?"

"Run it. Or find someone who can. There's just one caveat."

"There always is," Maile said. Auntie had found a sore spot on the sole of Maile's foot and was grinding a knuckle into it.

"There's a matter of back taxes that need to be paid."

"And since the bar is in my name, I'm responsible for paying them?"

"That's the idea."

"How much?" she asked.

"Three years' worth. But the good news about that is that since Robbie was such a terrible businessman, there was never much profit. In fact, it looks like there might be more expenses out of your pocket than profits. I'm having one of our tax experts looking it over right now."

"I can't afford too many experts looking at things, David. And yes, I know that sounds pretty silly since I'm splurging on a massage."

"Don't worry about it. There's more good news."

Maile's rear end, thighs, calves, and feet had been thoroughly massaged, stretched, and abused by then, and Auntie was beginning to work on her shoulders. "In two minutes or less, what is it?"

"I got a letter from the state board of licensing. They've reinstated your RN license, effective immediately."

Maile lifted her head, but it was pushed down again. "That's great! But I thought there needed to be a hearing about it?"

Auntie undid the knot in Maile's hair and let it free before starting a neck massage.

"I sent them a letter on your behalf. That's all they needed, a detailed explanation of what happened the evening of the trouble at the hospital. I got that from the accounts you gave to the hospital, to your old lawyer, and to my office. I was able to use all of it as evidence."

Maile celebrated internally. "Yes, my old lawyer was pretty useless. Does that mean I can finally get a real job?"

"Give it a couple more days until the state's website reflects the changes, but yes. There shouldn't be any changes or notes about licensure gaps, either."

"That's something, I guess. It's been a year since I worked as a nurse. I'll have to compete with new grads for a job. I wish I could get that pay back."

"It looks like you will. I've already been talking to the hospital about it. When I informed them that we're considering a wrongful dismissal lawsuit, they said something about paying all your back pay for the year, along with benefits that were lost."

David was full of surprises. Here was another one. "I didn't know I was considering a lawsuit?"

"Of course you are!" David said cheerfully. "If it's okay with you, I'll pursue a settlement."

Maile was on good news overload, which was being balanced by the scalp massage that was being inflicted on her head by Auntie's knuckles. She gave David permission and ended the call.

"Are you almost done?" she asked Auntie.

"Okay, done!"

Maile realized her muscles were even sorer at the end than they had been at the beginning of the massage. Blood was rushing through her body, giving her a warm, glowy sensation. When she lay there trying to separate pain from pleasure, Auntie started making a new knot in her hair.

"That's okay, I can do that," Maile said, sitting on the edge of the massage bench.

"Hair very long."

Maile started winding it. "Yep."

"Want haircutty?"

"Not today, thanks. I have somewhere to go."

"Not much time. Go fast."

"Not today." It was the same thing as always, that whenever she went to a salon for nails, a stylist would proposition her for much more, making all sorts of promises of how glamorous she'd look at the end. Maile thought of Ota's suggestion to make some changes to her appearance in an attempt to disguise her looks while out in public, but it was too late to do anything that day. She slipped down to the floor and stuffed her feet in her cork wedges and snugged the straps. "When I decide, I promise I'll come back here."

Auntie didn't seem to understand, but smiled anyway.

Chapter Four

It was only a twenty-minute walk from Chinatown to the palace and statue downtown, and Maile felt every pound of her weight on the soles of her feet as she walked. The knots and kinks that Auntie had worked on were relaxing a little more with each step she took. By the time she got to the State Supreme Court building near the Iolani Palace, she felt re-energized.

Watching as Lopaka drew the tour van to a stop near Kamehameha's statue across from the Iolani Palace, Maile finished her sandwich, and rinsed her mouth with water to wash down her breath mint. She smiled brightly while her guests filed off the bus, greeting them one by one. They were Australian kids, tweenies and teenagers, all dressed alike in green and yellow athletic team clothing. Not many of them looked particularly athletic, though. But like all teens everywhere, they were energetic. Once they were busy snapping pictures of everything in sight, she took Lopaka to one side.

"Eh brah. How're my teeth?"

Lopaka looked when she grinned widely. He pointed. "Maybe one kind uku."

Maile picked at her teeth. "Where?"

"No, other side."

She picked again and flushed more water. "Get it?"

"Made it worse. Got more of them now."

Hoping he was teasing her, she tossed her bottle of water onto her seat in the van. "Lolo, you know that?"

Lopaka laughed. "You sound like my wife."

Maile checked her itinerary before watching her guests for a moment. "For some reason, I just can't get enthused about today."

"We're here several times a week. It's bound to get boring after a while." Lopaka glanced at Maile for a second. "I didn't mean it to sound that way. You know how I feel about the Palace, and its history, Mai."

"I know, brah. I'm not bored with the tours. It's just something about this tour today that isn't sitting right. I have an odd feeling about it."

"What kind of odd?" he asked.

"Like something's going to get broken, or one of them will sprain an ankle running up the stairs. Bloody nose, lost camera, late for the potty. Something's going to happen. I know it."

"Their parents needed to sign waivers, or Thomas wouldn't have let them book the kid on the tour."

Maile shivered, even though the afternoon was warm. "All the waivers in the world won't cover my butt if something really stupid happens to a kid."

They checked their printed itineraries again.

"Ten Australian teenaged historians for a deluxe behind the scenes tour of the Iolani Palace," he said. "What can go wrong with that?"

"A lot." Maile looked at the kids waiting for the tour to start. A couple of them were flirting a little too aggressively for her tastes. One of the girls was checking her face with a tiny mirror. Two others were gossiping about someone else. And a boy with a bad case of acne was standing alone, pushing a pebble around the pavement with his toe. Two boys had started a game of hacky sack. She was already privately assigning them nicknames. "Shouldn't they be at the beach?"

She had to reframe the tour she was about to give for kids, rather than for adults. She'd never felt comfortable giving tours to kids, and today she was faced with a group of them, and without parental chaperones. She knew how much trouble they could be, and once one kid started in on shenanigans, the others we sure to follow. With a shrug of her shoulders, and one last sweep of her teeth with her tongue, she went out to greet them.

"So, you all know each other, right?"

"Yes, Miss Spencer," the tallest girl said. "Minus one. Janet had to bail. She's a little crook today."

"Missed her brekky," a boy said. He seemed rather pleased with himself that there was trouble for one of them.

"Defo taking a sickie. Me mate. I should know."

It was a 'Huh?' moment for Maile. It sounded like they were speaking English, but weren't. She assumed there was one less kid going on the tour. It turned out that the one that didn't make the trip was named Janet. It was also painfully obvious she and Lopaka were the only adults on the tour. Each of the kids was the Australian stereotype, with blond hair, blue eyes, a few freckles, and perfect teeth. In a couple more years, they could be making advertisements for Crazy Shirts, surf wear, and hair bleach.

"I'd appreciate it if you called me Maile," she told them.

Malice at the Palace

"No, Miss Spencer," the tallest girl said. "We have to address our teachers as Mister, Missus, or Miss. It's a rule."

"First of all, I'm not one of your teachers and this isn't a classroom."

"It is to us, Miss Spencer," one of the littler kids said.

Another girl put her hand up. "This is an official class activity."

A headache was already starting and Maile wondered if she had aspirin in her bag. "Okay, fine. Call me Ms. Spencer."

"We don't use that term at our school, Miss Spencer. It's either Miss or Missus."

"Miss," Maile said, forcing a smile while stretching the hissing sound.

After telling them about the statue of Kamehameha, and why so many lei hung from his out-stretched arm and adorned the pedestal of the statue, she spoke about her hometown as they walked around the Supreme Court building.

"Honolulu doesn't have the usual downtown with giant skyscrapers that most American cities have. Most high-rises here are in Waikiki. But it's very pleasant to go for a stroll down here, if you come back. Where do you come from in Australia?"

"We're Margies," one of the boys said.

"Margie?"

"He means we come from Margaret River in Western Australia. Have you been there?" the tall girl asked. Her name was fittingly Margo. Maybe she was taking pity on Maile by not using Australian slang.

"Never been to Australia. Maybe someday. What is Margaret River famous for?"

"Cow Bombie."

"Huh?"

"Big waves," a young girl said. "Just a small town, but we're famous for wines and caves."

"Oh, so you're surfers?" Maile asked, hoping she'd found something to talk about.

"Us? Forget it. We're readers," Margo said. "We're all in the reading and history clubs at school."

"That's interesting," Maile said, as Lopaka leaned against the van nearby reading a magazine. She tried positioning herself to see across the busy thoroughfare at the Palace, but there was too much traffic and trees blocking her view. Ota had said something about a protest there today, and she wondered if it had started yet. Picketers waving signs and flags weren't a very good introduction to a tourist site. "Are they big clubs?"

"Just us. Surf Club's the biggest." Margo kept talking about the clubs at school, almost sounding as if she were homesick.

Maile barely paid attention, instead watching a group of people coming down the sidewalk before turning in the front entrance gate to the Palace. They were carrying flags and picket signs, but she couldn't see what they said. It wasn't uncommon for fringe Hawaiian secessionist groups to protest at the palace, demanding the return of the islands to native islanders. There was a core group that protested most often, and she knew most of those participants by name. For the most part, she stayed away from those protests, even though her heart often ached for more recognition of Hawaiian people from the federal government. From where she was, she couldn't see their faces to see if it was the usual crowd.

She gave the kids a talk about the Hawaii State Supreme Court building, of how it was built in the same American Florentine architectural style as the Iolani Palace.

"In the Hawaiian language, it's called Ali'iolani Hale, or House of Heavenly Kings. Something you kids might be interested in knowing it that it was designed by an Australian to be Kamehameha the Fifth's royal palace." Maile watched as more protesters went down the sidewalk to the entrance of the Palace across the street. "As soon as the building was done, he allowed it to be used for government offices." What Maile had never understood was why protesters didn't bring their picket signs and banners to that building. "It's still a working federal office building, and the site where in 1983, Queen Lili'uokalani and her monarchy were overthrown by public proclamation. After that, those federal offices were moved to the Palace that we'll visit in a few minutes, which quickly housed the provisional government of the Republic of Hawaii."

Maile did her best to give a talk about the Queen's trial and imprisonment in the Palace without turning it into a lecture—or a rant. She let them mill around and take a few more pictures of the building. It was just about time to go to the Palace, where she'd have to give the same talk all over again, only making it sound different.

"What's that all about?" she asked Lopaka quietly, watching a few more people go through the gate. One of them was banging a drum to get attention, while the others shouted slogans.

"Just a bunch of nuts. Want me to take you in another gate?"

"So much nicer going in the main entrance. It seems regal somehow. I feel like I'm sneaking in using the Kinau gate."

"What about the Likelike gate?"

"The one used by the royal family back then? Forget it. Anyway, I start my tour at the front."

He snickered. "Yeah, don't want to mix up pages of your script."

"Script's been memorized for a long time now. As long as we go in the front door, I can give the tour blindfolded."

Maile noticed tourists on foot that were aiming for the main entrance, but when they saw the noisy group on the palace grounds, they went off in search of another way in.

Lopaka drove them through the main gate known as the Kauikeaouli gate, the one used for ceremonial purposes. That's where the protesters had congregated, as they usually did, in the large area directly in front of the steps up to the main entrance. That was considered the front of the building, one of the most photographed sites in the islands. Today, it was being photographed with dozens of protesters waving signs and flags. As Lopaka eased the tour van along, picketers slapped the side of it with signs and hands, getting their point across.

"Miss Spencer…" Margo said in a whiny voice.

"Don't worry about them. They show up here from time to time."

"Are the coppers coming?" a boy asked. He was busy snapping pictures out his window as though he were a junior journalist.

"Coppers? Oh. Hopefully, the police won't need to come today."

Maile dug through her bag for the bottle of aspirin she kept. It was empty. Going to second best, she chewed a couple of antacid tablets.

"You okay?" Lopaka asked.

"Bob's your uncle," she said back.

"Huh?"

"I don't know what I'm talking about." She took off her narrating headset and tossed it aside. "Nicest kids in the world and I can't understand a word they're saying."

As usual, they parked off to one side to take advantage of the shade. The picketers followed. Once the van was stopped, it was surrounded by what was turning into a small but angry mob.

"Miss Spencer? Why are they yelling at us?" Margo asked.

"I'm not sure why," she muttered, still trying to read a few of the signs. The shouting, like the signs, was in both Hawaiian and in English. When several of them spotted her at the front of the van, they gathered there, still banging hands and posters on the van. Then she was able to read a few of the signs, and wished she hadn't. "I don't like the looks of this."

"Why are they so mad at us?" one of the boys asked.

"They're not mad at you. They seem to be upset with me."

Maile go home! one of their signs said.

No more Hawaiian wahine-kamali'i!
Go home haole girl Maile Spencer!

Another sign had a hand-drawn image of a falling star. *Hokuhoku'ikalani no more wanted here!*

"What the heck, brah?" she asked Lopaka. "What's this all about?"

"They're lolo, Mai. Don't listen to them."

The picketers had begun to walk circles around the van, chanting a slogan. The kids were watching out their windows, a few laughing, others looking nervous.

"What's going on, Miss Spencer?" Margo asked.

"Well, native Hawaiians hold protests every now and then. They usually aren't so rambunctious as this, though."

"They're going to do that all day?"

"Usually not. Once the day gets hot, they'll wander off."

"Isn't that your name?" one kid asked.

"Um, yeah. They seem to be upset with me."

"Defo not happy about something. We're still going on the tour?"

When a couple of the women began banging their hands on the side of the bus, demanding Maile to get off, Lopaka went out to confront them. While he did that, Maile got her phone and dialed a number she had saved in her primary number list.

"Detective Ota, this is Maile Spencer. I have a problem."

"If it's about Prince Aziz…"

"Not about him. The protests you mentioned at the Palace have already started."

"What's going on?"

"I'm surrounded by protestors wanting a piece of me."

"Piece of what part?"

"From the looks on their faces, anything that bleeds. Is there something that can be done?"

"If they're threatening your safety, get back on the bus and call 9-1-1."

"We haven't been off yet. They have me and my guests trapped on the bus. Lopaka is out there arguing with some of them, which isn't going well, and someone else just threw a banana peel at the windshield. Others are looking a little too aggressive with their sign waving. Are they allowed to do this with the permit you gave them?"

"I didn't give them the permit, a clerk did. And no, they're not allowed to be violent. Do you recognize any of them?"

"I know a few from church." A tomato hit the window next to her. "Not that church sermons have done them much good when it comes to brotherly love."

"Make a list of the people you recognize."

"Should I take their pictures?" she asked.

"No. That'll just make matters worse. Let me call you back in about five minutes," he said.

It felt like the longest five minutes of her life while Maile waited for the HPD police detective to call back.

"I don't know if it's good news or bad, but they're the ones I told you about earlier and have a proper permit to be there today. The permit is for today only, though, and only outside. They're not allowed to impede the entrance or business of others in any way."

"Impede the entrance?" Maile wanted to laugh. "They're not letting me out of the tour bus."

"Where's Lopaka?" Ota asked.

"Still outside arguing with the picketers. He's been snapping some of the picket signs over his knee."

"If they let him out, they might let you out. Do you have visitors with you?"

"Nine kids from Australia. Not having a Honolulu Chamber of Commerce moment right now."

"Maile, just open the door and tell them to get out of the way, and that if any of them touches you or your guests, you'll call the police to have them arrested. In fact, I already have a squad car on the way. They should be there any minute. Your boyfriend, Brock, by the way."

"Not my boyfriend. I have enough trouble without people making up lies about me."

"What're they protesting, anyway?" Ota asked.

"Me."

Malice at the Palace

Chapter Five

When Maile's foot touched down to asphalt, two protesters were in her ears, one on each side of her. She barely heard their words, but the intent came through loud and clear. Most of it was how she was no longer considered their princess, a quiet leader of the community, and that she had betrayed Hawaiians and their culture. When she asked what she had betrayed, she didn't get a clear answer, only that she was being selfish. Lopaka kept arguing the entire time, pulling people away from Maile and her group of kids so they'd have a clear path to the steps up to the front entrance. Once they got there, the picketers remained on the ground level where they belonged, never once committing any act that might be considered illegal.

"They're smart enough not to follow us," Lopaka said.

"Probably because they've been arrested before." She started nudging the kids toward the door. "Let's get the tour started before anything else happens."

Instead of starting her tour on the porch outside as usual, she took the kids inside for the quiet. Holding the door and counting each one as they went in, she noticed three full-sized luxury SUVs pull into the parking area and stop. Right behind them came a police squad car that parked to the other side. Brock Turner got out of that and went straight to the picketers, confronting them. All that accomplished was to start another argument. On his heels came a sedan, this vehicle she recognized. It was

Detective Ota who emerged. He went to the picketers, joining Officer Turner and Lopaka in confronting them.

She watched the SUVs, all black with tinted windows gleaming in the sunshine, and nothing happened. No one got out, and Ota seemed to ignore them. They apparently weren't police or they'd get out and help quiet the picketers. Maybe they were VIPs there for a private tour of their own. Maile didn't recognize the vehicles and there were no signs or logos on them that they might be from a rival tour company. All she could figure was that some sort of politician was visiting, and once that private tour started, Maile and her group would get pushed out of the way.

"Whatever," she said, letting the heavy door close behind her. She corralled the kids to start he talk.

"Those people sure don't like you much," one boy said.

"What was that all about?" Margo asked.

"I'm not exactly sure. It might have something to do with some Hawaiian artifacts that were stolen recently, and those people might be thinking I had something to do with it."

"Did you?"

"The artifacts have been returned and the thieves have been arrested. The last I heard, they're awaiting trial. But what happened outside doesn't happen very often and is definitely not a part of today's tour."

"Why are they mad about that?" Margo asked. She was turning out to be the group spokesperson.

"They might've heard that I was the one who returned the artifacts." Maile tried to square her mind,

Malice at the Palace

trying to find the words that would start the tour. "Honestly, I don't know what they're thinking."

"Do we still get to go on the tour?" Margo asked.

"Of course!" Maile pointed with her hand, inviting them to move forward into the main hall. "Please, let's get started."

She discussed the modern cushioned carpeting that stretched from one end of the grand hall to the staircase on the ground floor, along with the polished koa wood, much it still original to the large building, more than a hundred years old.

"You can see the portraits of past monarchs of the Islands. Can anyone name one or two?" she asked.

All nine kids raised their hands. The youngest, a tweenie-aged girl named Irene, correctly named the ones they could see from where they stood.

"That's very good! Have you been studying our kings and queens?"

"We all have," Margo said. "Each year, we pick a place to visit and learn its history before going there. It's a school project for the history club."

"Wow. It sounds like you guys are experts. Maybe you should give me the tour?"

The kids laughed.

"We wanted to have a tour from someone with inside knowledge about the Iolani Palace. That's why we wanted you, Miss Spencer."

"Why do you think I have inside information about the palace?"

"We've been reading blogs," a boy named Noah said. He was skinny, with a bad complexion, and had an impossibly long neck. "There was one written by a yank named Sam Gee. You know her?"

"Sam Gee?" Maile couldn't think of any men she'd given tours to lately with a name like that.

"A girl in some mid-western state," Margo added.

"Oh, Sammy Gibson. Yes, she's visited here a couple of times. She wrote a blog post about her vacation in Hawaii? That's nice."

"The whole blog is about Hawaii, and one entire post was all about you, how you're an authentic Hawaiian princess. That's what made us want to come here this year."

For the second time that day, Maile tried not to laugh at how others perceived her. "I'm not so sure how big of a deal it is."

"Sure seemed like it to those people out there," Margo said.

"Well, I'm not the Queen Mother, or whatever she's called in England." Maile led the group to the first room on her tour.

"We went to England two years ago. We didn't come anywhere near meeting royalty then. Just saw a bunch of dusty old paintings of them."

"Kind of like seeing these painting in here today?" Maile asked.

"But you're real. You really are a princess, right?" Irene asked.

"Yes, I suppose in some sort of official capacity I am. But not much comes with the title, except getting yelled at by protestors occasionally."

On the fringe of the group, two boys were playing some sort of game. Maile recognized it as rock, paper, scissors, and it was being played in a physically ambitious way. Maile decided to keep positioned near them while on the tour, just in case any trouble started.

"That's why it's so exciting meeting you, Miss Spencer," Irene said. "A real princess."

She chanced taking her eyes off the boys. "Oh, well, thanks."

"Sam Gee said you have another name, what was it?" Margo asked her friends. "Hoku…"

Irene put her hand up. "Hokuhoku'ikalani."

"It means bright star in the sky," someone else said.

"Very good. You really have been studying." She was impressed, and maybe a little concerned, with how knowledgeable they were about Hawaiian history, and with her. Somehow, she needed to redirect them back to the Palace tour. "In each of the wall niches are statues or pottery that go back to the days of the kingdom, gifts from other monarchs, from Europe, Japan, and India. Quite beautiful, and I suppose priceless. You'll notice a chair in front of each blocking someone from getting too close. That includes all of us."

Almost as if on cue, the two rambunctious boys bumped into a chair. One of them fell into it, his head swinging back and bumping a tall vase. Maile got to it before it could fall.

"Oliver! David!" shrieked Margo like a mother hen. "What did I tell the two of you about that?"

"Yes, it might be best for everybody if the athletic stuff is kept for outside," Maile said, leading them away. "If everyone behaves themselves, I promise to show you a haunted tree here on the grounds at the end of the tour."

"Haunted as in ghosts?"

"Haunted as in spirits of the people who have resided in this building. But that'll be later." She steered them into a room. "This is the Blue Room. As you can see, it's draped and upholstered in blues, and has more portraits of our latest queens and kings."

Maile was off the hook for having to tell much about the rooms or furnishings, since the kids had done so much research on the place before they came. To take advantage of the break, she found the docent that had met them at the entrance.

"Mrs. Goodwin, would you mind watching the kids for five minutes while I do something?" Maile asked. She tried her best not to notice her past history schoolteacher's bright blond hair, obviously dyed all one color. It had been the same when Maile was in her classes over a decade before. It didn't fool anyone then, even if it did hide white hairs the way her makeup was meant to hide a few crow's feet and laugh lines. Now that she was retired and volunteering as a palace docent, Maile was always glad to see the woman on her tours.

"Of course. You have your offering?"

Maile displayed the plastic box that contained the lei she'd brought in her bag, something ordinarily off-limits in the building.

"You're always discreet. You realize we have to collect it at the end of the day, right?"

"That's what I figured. I'll just be a couple of minutes, I promise."

Maile hurried to the end of the Grand Hall and ducked into the Throne Room. Taking the plastic box from her bag, she got the maile vine lei she'd bought that

Malice at the Palace

morning and hung it over the armrest of the Queen's throne. Taking two steps back, she whispered a prayer for Queen Kapiolani and King Kalakaua, the past users of those thrones.

Mrs. Goodwin was just bringing the kids into the throne room when Maile was finishing her petitions to any god that was listening right then. Most of her requests were about whatever might've been going on with the protesters outside the palace.

While she gave a short but somewhat grandiose lecture about the queen and king that had last used that room, she heard voices come from the Grand Hall. All men, it didn't sound as though they were interested in seeing any of the downstairs rooms, but went straight upstairs. That was the living area of past monarchs, and was closely monitored by docents. They didn't sound like protestors, probably the VIP tour group from the SUVs, so she didn't pay them much mind, only continuing with her own tour.

After an hour on the lower floor, she took the group upstairs for the second half of the tour. The first place they went was to the Imprisonment Room. She continued the story of how Queen Lili'uokalani had been arrested for trying to restore the Hawaiian monarchy, and then tried in the throne room.

"Found guilty of basically nothing, she was confined to this room for eight months," Maile told the group. The two boys that had come close to breaking an invaluable vase downstairs were secretly discussing something hidden in the palm of a hand. Keeping up her lesson about the queen, she edged around the group to get a better look at what the boys had. As they snickered,

Maile crept closer. They must not have noticed her, because they started a game of hacky sack. On the third kick, she reached out to catch the footbag in mid-air. Before they could complain, she dropped it in a pocket, all while keeping up her lesson. "Odd how people can be imprisoned for just the slightest error in judgment."

Maile led them in a circle around the room, stopping at the quilt that was on display beneath glass.

Even the boys had settled down by then, listening intently as they made a circle around the display. Being such a personal thing made by Hawaii's last queen, it was one of Maile's favorite spots to visit in the entire palace. "During the time of her imprisonment, the Queen was allowed only one visitor, her lady in waiting. All Lili'uokalani could do to pass the time was read, compose music, and make this quilt."

"Miss Spencer," Irene said, raising her hand again. "Why isn't there anything in this room? Just the quilt."

"When the last of the monarchs, the rightful inhabitants of the palace, were forced to leave, the building became a government office building for many years. In those early days, they decided the homey furnishings weren't useful as office furniture, so most of it was sold. The palace is still trying to recover lost pieces of artwork and furniture that once decorated these rooms."

"Do they get much back?"

"Every now and then, a piece is discovered and returned. It's so infrequent that when something authentic is found, it becomes a news item."

While the boys inspected woodwork and the girls gazed at the colorful quilt, Maile and Margo strolled around the room. They stopped at a window and Maile looked outside. Both Officer Turner's and Detective Ota's cars were gone, and even the protesters had found a place in the shade to sit and eat lunch. The three SUVs were parked in the shade of banyan trees, one man in dark clothes and sunglasses hanging around them as though he was some sort of a guard, smoking a cigarette.

"When we went to England that time…" Margo said. "…we all thought were going to meet the Queen while on a tour of Buckingham Palace. Never once did she show her face. Then we found out she was at Balmoral."

"I'm not real familiar with England," Maile said.

"The palaces and museums there are chock full of stuff. I doubt they even know half that stuff is there. It's like they get something and go off to look for an empty space to put it."

Maile almost felt jealous. Almost. But just like all of her life, she wouldn't have traded her heritage for anything, even if she was only 25% Hawaiian.

They had an hour left of the tour and one last room to visit. She'd been having fun with the teens, even if there were a couple of near-misses with palace furnishings and an unauthorized athletic contest.

"Well, we have one last room to view, and it might be the most interesting to the boys. It's King Kalakaua's bedroom, and one of the best furnished of all the rooms. Please do not enter the room or stand on the rug. We can only view it from the doorway, so you'll have to crowd together a little and take turns looking."

When they got to the room, two men were standing outside the door. They were dressed in dark colors and had on overcoats, odd for the tropics. That convinced Maile that there was a VIP tour still in progress. Honolulu was a popular place to visit and to hold conferences, and the Iolani Palace was a major stop on anyone's itinerary. It could be something of a thrill for the kids, to possibly meet someone they might've seen on TV news.

Neither guard bothered stepping aside when they got to the doorway. With a closer look to their faces, she could see they were all business. Their skin was dark, facial stubble heavy, and attitudes unyielding. While one looked down at Maile with a sneer, the other scanned the kids.

"You mind?" Maile said. She could also be unyielding, even if the other guest was somehow more important than hers. "We just want to take a look inside the room."

Both men continued to look at her, almost glaring. Maile shook her head over the men's impoliteness. That still didn't move them aside.

Someone behind the guards spoke in a foreign language, something that sounded like a command. That finally made the men step aside, but not by much. The kids crowded past the men for a better look into the room. Since she had most of the room put to memory, Maile decided to remain back from the doorway to give her talk. The two bodyguards seemed much more interested in watching her than the kids.

"King Kalakaua was a fan of new technology, which explains why there's a telephone here in his bedroom. It was one of the first phones in Hawaii. These days, we all have phones in our pockets wherever we go.

Malice at the Palace

Speaking of going places, the king had furnishings and decorations from all over the world. He was especially fond of Asian and European pieces. Maybe a few of those decorations look similar to what you saw at Buckingham Palace?"

Maile had a secret game she played on tours of the Palace. While the kids looked through the doorway whispering to each other, Maile wondered how she would decorate a room in the palace for herself. She smiled to herself, that even though she was related to the past occupants many times removed, history books and tours were as close as she'd ever get to living like royalty.

When her phone rang, she slipped it from a pocket in her skirt. The caller was David Melendez. Seeing the kids still keenly interested in what was in the room and taking turns to look, she stepped away to take the call.

"I'm right in the middle of a tour, David. Make it quick."

"Done deal with your license. I just checked and it's live on the state's website. You can go get a real job again."

Maile noticed a few of the boys snickering over whatever it was they were gazing at. "Halleluiah. But you didn't have to call me for that."

"Other good news. The hospital is willing to settle."

"And once again, I'm glad, but you could've waited until tomorrow to tell me that. I survive on tip money from these tours, which means all my attention needs to be on them and not on phone calls."

"Forget your tip money. You'll want to hear this. They made an offer before I could even make a demand.

Not only are they willing to pay back wages and bennies, but they're slapping a million dollars on top of that."

The blood drained from her face. "Huh?"

"If they're willing to pay that much so easily, I bet I could get two million out of them."

Maile took another step away from her group. "Wait. They want to give me how much?"

"A million, plus lost wages. But there'd be an NDA for you to sign. Would you?"

"Non-Disclosure Agreement? Of course, if I got the same from them. That'd be important, right? You're the lawyer. I don't know about these things."

"I can get everything squared away so you're protected. Do you want me to try for more?"

"No!" Maile turned around to see her group beginning to back away from the doorway at the insistence of the two men there. "Just take whatever they offer. I don't want this to turn into an ordeal. I just want to be done with Honolulu Med."

"They also made some noise that if you ever applied for a job there, your application would somehow get lost."

"I figured as much. I have other employment ideas that I'm pursuing anyway." She noticed the Hacky Sack Kids discussing something with the men at the door, and it looked like it was going in an impolite direction. "I have to go. Give me a call when all the forms need to be signed."

Without looking at her phone, she ended the call and put it in her pocket. She got the group together again and led them down the hall to wrap up her tour.

"What about the guys inside the room?" one of the Hacky Sack Kids asked. She'd heard their names at one point but couldn't remember them right then.

"Guys?" Maile wondered if some restoration work was being done. "What guys?"

"The chaps standing around."

"Another is in the bed."

"He's not in the bed, he's on it, Trevor. Get it right."

"On the bed. What's the big diff?"

Maile was even more confused. Had the palace decided to put mannequins on display? She pushed her way through the kids and the men to the doorway to see for herself what they were talking about. What she found put her in a state of speechlessness.

Chapter Six

Maile pushed past the two guards. She unclasped the velvet rope that was meant to prohibit entry and flung it aside. Almost running, she went to the side of the bed where a man was stretched out on top of the royal quilt that adorned the bed. It wasn't just any quilt, but one with the Hawaiian royal coat of arms stitched into it.

"Get off that bed!" When the man didn't move, she raised her voice. "What do you think you're doing? Get off that bed, I said!"

The man in a long white Arab's gown and white headdress had his head propped up on two pillows, his hand clasped behind his head. He simply smiled back at Maile.

The kids had followed her, and were making 'Uh-oh!' noises. Otherwise, the room was silent.

"I told you to get off that bed!"

Someone else ran into the room. Maile glanced over her shoulder to see the docent in a panic. Mrs. Goodwin didn't shake easily, but her face was as white as a ghost. A man had followed her, not one of the grim dark-skinned bodyguards, but a white man with a wired ear bud in one ear. He was pressing it in and nodding in response to whoever was speaking to him.

"What's going on?" the man asked, looking more at Maile than anyone else.

"That's what I'd like to know!" Maile said, trying not to shout. "Who are you and why is he on that bed?"

Malice at the Palace

He took Maile by the arm. "We should talk out in the hall."

She shook off his grip. "I want answers!"

"Don't you recognize me, Miss Spencer?" the Middle Eastern man on the bed asked. "Or is it Princess Maile?"

"I know exactly who you are. You belong in prison! Get off that bed this instant!"

"I think I'll stay in this room. I'm quite comfortable here, even though it's such a small room."

"I said..." She grabbed his sleeve and began to pull. "...get off that bed!"

For as quiet as it was in Kalakaua's bedroom, she was able to hear a click before she felt a hard tapping on the back of her head. When she looked behind her, she found one of the men from outside the door had come in. He was holding a giant pistol-like gun, aimed directly at her.

"You will not touch the Prince," he said in broken English.

"I...this isn't...he's not supposed to be..."

"You no make rules here," the dark-skinned man said slowly through pursed lips. "Prince Aziz make rules here."

"This isn't..." She noticed the gun again, steady in the man's hand. "He's not..."

"I'm afraid he's right," the white man said in American accented English. Maile took a longer look at him, now that a gun had her attention. He was occidental looking, with light hair and pale skin, and was wearing dark, tactical military clothing. He had on what looked like a bulletproof vest, and a large boxy handgun

55

attached to it. He was familiar, and she might've been able to figure out who he was if panic hadn't been crowding her mind.

"That bed is for the king! Not that guy! He isn't…" She began pulling at the man on the bed again, but stopped when she was reminded a gun was aimed at her.

"He isn't what, Miss Spencer?" the white man asked. "Royal enough to be in this room?"

"He isn't…" Maile assessed this new fellow for a moment, trying desperately to make sense of what was happening. Behind the bodyguards, Mrs. Goodwin looked ready to faint, while the Australian kids had a mixture of looks to their faces ranging from excited, to panic, to close to tears, to ready to laugh at the show. Maile still struggled to find a name that went with the man's face. "He's not Hawaiian and this is not the Prince's palace."

"But you admit he is a prince?"

"I don't know. I guess in Khashraq he is."

"And this is the royal bedroom meant for a man?"

"It was King Kalakaua's bedroom! Not his," she said, nodding at the Middle Eastern prince stretched out on the King's bed. "Why is he on the bed?"

"Prince Aziz has decided to move into the palace. He likes this room to be his bedroom."

"What do you mean, he's moving in here?" By now, Maile had forgotten all about the man in the bed behind her, and the guns. She put her hands on her hips and glared at the American in front of her. "Now I remember you. You're that handyman who put locks on my door a while back. Jeff something."

"Very good!"

Malice at the Palace

Maile shifted her eyes back and forth between him and the prince on the bed, her mind slowly figuring things out. "Now I get it. That's how those kahili got into my room a while back. You had extra keys to let him in. But why? Who's he to you?"

"My employer. I'm in charge of the Prince's bodyguards."

"I don't care about that. I want to know what's going on! Why is he moving in here?"

Before Jeff could answer, Prince Aziz traded a few words in Arabic with a bodyguard. He nodded, and whispered into Jeff's ear, who translated for Maile.

"The Prince is tired. He'd like to be left alone now."

"I don't care what he is!"

Jeff clamped his large hand around Maile's arm to pull her away. "It might be best if we left him alone."

"Take her to the Throne Room, along with the others," Prince Aziz said. "I'll be down after I've rested."

"The Throne Room? What's going on here?" Maile continued to demand as she was taken from the room. By then, two more bodyguards had shown up outside the door.

The group of Australian kids was led down while Maile was held back. Her hands were tied behind her back with a cord, she was blindfolded with a bandana, and she was patted down. Her phone was taken from her pocket and dropped in her bag, which was also taken from her. The hacky sack footbag was found, examined, and put back in her pocket. With that, she was pushed along a few feet behind the kids toward the Throne Room.

What had always brought Maile a sense of pride while walking through the Palace, now gave her a sense of foreboding. The usual creaks in the wooden stairs were quiet. Voices barely made sense. Unable to see where she was going, a hand clamped to her arm pulled her along. The trip seemed long, almost tiresome.

Once in the Throne Room, Maile listened as someone gave instructions in Arabic to others. Margo spoke up, telling her friends to sit down. Trying to make sense of what they were doing, Maile imagined the room with windows was a long row of upright chairs upholstered in red velvet, prized antiques that were for display only. During what sounded like a game of musical chairs, each kid found a place to sit, and once they had settled, they were told to remain quiet. With that, two of the girls began to cry.

Not knowing what else to do, Maile tried placing the position of everybody in the room.

"What did I tell you?" one girl said to no one in particular. "I told you we'd have problems on a tour today."

Margo answered her. "Yes, Evie, we should've heeded your premonition, but it's too late now."

There were heavy footsteps before Jeff spoke. "What's this about a premonition?"

"That's all Evie talked about at brekky, that we were going to have bad luck today." Margo seemed to laugh nervously. "And look what we've found."

"Just keep her quiet," Jeff said, his heavy footsteps walking away.

"I'm sorry, Margo, Evie," Maile said from where she stood across the room.

"That guy upstairs isn't a part of the tour?" a boy asked.

"The only tour he should be on is of the shower room at the federal penitentiary," Maile hissed.

"That kind of talk will only get you in trouble," Jeff told her.

"Like I already don't have trouble?"

"Just be quiet."

"Don't tell me to be quiet."

She listened to more footsteps until someone was standing right in front of her.

"Be smart about this, Miss Spencer. Don't cause yourself trouble you can't get out of." Jeff spoke Arabic to a couple of the bodyguards, and footsteps left the room. That left only him and one other Middle Eastern bodyguard present, as far as Maile knew. "Find a seat."

"Where?"

"Use a throne," he said. He began to pull her to one side.

She stopped like a tired mule. "No."

"One way or another, you're going to sit."

"Take the blindfold off and I'll sit."

"And be quiet?"

"Forget that." She gave the negotiation some thought. "Maybe I won't be noisy."

Jeff pulled the blindfold down so it rested on her shoulders.

"That can go back on at any time," he said.

When Maile looked at what was in front of her, she noticed the maile lei she'd left on the Queen's throne had been moved to the floor of the dais in front of the thrones. She went to the throne dais, crouched down, collected the lei in her bound hands, and hung it on the armrest again. Instead of sitting on the throne, she sat on one of the steps below.

"Can somebody please explain what's going on?" she asked, trying her best to keep the fear from her voice. She had an audience of nine teenagers that were looking to her for leadership. As it was, she'd lost track of Lopaka since they'd come in the entrance two hours before.

"Must be mystifying," Jeff said.

"A bit. Wouldn't it be to you, if you found someone taking up residence in an important home?"

"Such as the governor's mansion?"

"There's a difference between a governor and royalty, or even that of a president."

"Maybe so, but this is no longer a royal palace, and more of a museum," Jeff said.

Maile cocked her head slightly when looking back at the man. "Be very careful with what you say about this palace. You still haven't answered my question as to why you and that so-called prince are here."

"So called?" the Middle Eastern guard demanded after he strode to stand in front of her. He took up an aggressive posture, his legs apart, one hand on his gun. "Prince Aziz is proud Prince of Kingdom of Khashraq, and…"

Jeff gave him a pat on the back and sent him away with a message in Arabic. "Some of these guys get pretty uptight about their prince," he told Maile.

"He's not your prince, also?"

Malice at the Palace

"I'm just a privately contracted employee. Once this job is done, I won't care what happens to him, you, or anyone else on this island."

"Unfortunately, the rest of us have to live with the outcome of some weird prince's demands. Which I'm still not clear about. What exactly is going on here?"

"It's no coincidence that the Prince has come here on a day you're giving a tour."

"This invasion of Hawaiian territory was planned?" she asked.

"It's not an invasion, and of course it was planned, specifically for today."

"Men with guns taking over a royal palace sure sounds like an invasion to me. Or a coup. Is that what the Prince thinks he's doing? Taking the throne away from me? Because I have no more right or claim to these thrones than Prince Aziz does."

"Why do you think that?" Jeff asked.

"You just said it was planned. Someone moved the lei from the Queen's throne to the floor, as though the person who left it there had been somehow demoted. That would be me, Jeff. I'm the one who left it there."

"Um, pardon me, Miss Spencer?" Margo asked with her hand timidly raised. "A few of us need to use the loo."

"Okay, right now, it would be really helpful if we all spoke the same language."

"The restroom."

"It's downstairs."

"No one is going anywhere," the Middle Eastern gunman said.

Margo relayed a message from Evie, who'd quit crying. "We need to go pretty soon or there'll be a problem."

The gunman grinned. Maile had heard Jeff call him Omar. "Just go in clothes. Mommy won't care."

With that, Evie started crying again, along with Irene and a couple others.

"They're kids, Jeff. They've done what you've asked so far. At least let them go to the restroom."

"Who needs to go?" Jeff asked the kids while pacing a lap around the room. A few of them raised their hands. "Who needs to go worst?"

Evie's hand shot into the air as if she knew best.

"Okay, one at a time. No one else goes until the previous one comes back. And don't think about running for a door, because I have a man at each one."

Evie went first, leaving the room at a gallop.

"Okay, that little problem is in the process of being solved," Maile said. "Now, how about explaining to me what's going on? Why are we being held against our wills?"

"You are, naturally, aware of the legal trouble the prince is in?"

Maile watched as the Middle Eastern gunman lit a cigarette. "Does he need to do that? There's no smoking in this building."

Omar walked slowly back to where Maile sat on the dais. Taking a long drag, he blew it in her direction. "No smoking? Me? I smoke where I want."

"Not in here, you don't. Get rid of it."

He shrugged comically. "Where? I see no ashtray. Shall I drop on floor?"

Malice at the Palace

"Don't you dare!"

He held the smoldering cigarette out to take a long look at it. After one more drag, he bent over to be eye level with Maile. She watched as gray smoke came from his nostrils. Sweat was beading on his oily forehead. One drop of it was being held back from by a bushy eyebrow. When he grinned at her, he stuck the cigarette in her mouth.

"Don't let go of that. It'll burn the floor."

With the half-smoked cigarette clamped between her lips, Maile breathed through her nose while glaring at the man.

"It burns faster if you smoke it," Omar said, laughing.

Maile had a hard time keeping the smoke from her lungs, coughing slightly. That's when Jeff showed up. Taking the cigarette from Maile's mouth, he handed it back to Omar and told him to take it outside. Evie was just returning then, and Irene ran off to take her turn in the restroom.

"Getting back to the Prince," Jeff said. "Do you know how his trouble started?"

"Yes. I'm at the root of it, at least when it comes to his legal trouble. He's on trial for human trafficking of women, along with a few other things. That's the kind of man you're working for, if you can call that a man."

Irene came back and the next kid left, one of the Hacky Sack Kids, also in a rush. When Irene took her chair, she took up the pose of being the world's most polite child.

For once Jeff looked a little confused about what Maile had told him. "I don't particularly care why he's on trial. I only know he's moving in here to make a stand against what he's calling the tyranny and oppression of his status."

"Tyranny and oppression? Don't make me laugh! And what status is he supposed to be enjoying?"

"His diplomatic status as Prince of Khashraq."

"You know anything about Khashraq? Because what I've been reading about that place makes it sound not so great for the female of our species," Maile said.

One kid returned from the bathroom and another left.

"Look, it's clear he hasn't been getting a fair shake in his trial."

"What trial?" Maile tried to laugh. "One day of debating the charges and he was released again. I know, because I was there watching it all. And don't try and tell me there's been a trial in the media. Our government, the US government anyway, has kept the whole thing quiet, out of diplomatic respect for the Prince's kingdom."

"I've been told different."

"By who? And what he's been doing to women is fair? Your friend the Prince belongs behind bars, Jeff."

"All I know is that he's free on his own recognizance while the US District Attorney reloads her prosecution of him. Until his trial starts again, he's living here. I've been hired to make sure that happens."

"Why here?" Maile asked. "There are a dozen hotels in Waikiki that are far more luxurious and more comfortable than this building. This building isn't suitable to live in. Just like you said earlier, it's no longer a palace, but a museum. There's not much of a kitchen, only a small room for employees and docents to eat their lunch. There's no staff here to take care of him. Why here?"

"It's a royal palace."

"Yes, the only one in America. That's what he wants, to take over a royal palace?" she asked. "Why doesn't he go to a country with a real working monarchy for that?"

"It's America, and how he's being treated here, that he has problems with. Why is it, Miss Spencer, that you have issues with the Prince staying here for a few days?"

"This isn't the first time we've met here. All he did that time was insult the place, how his personal palace at home is so much better." One kid returned, another left for the restroom. So far as Maile could see, there hadn't been any accidents on antique furniture. "It's the federal government that has problems with the Prince, not me. If it were up to me, he'd be gone. Let someone else deal with the jerk. I don't care anymore."

"What about all those poor, oppressed women your heart was just bleeding over?" Jeff asked. "Don't you care about them?"

Maile glared at him. "Don't press that button, pal, because it's a game you won't win. Maybe you'll win today's skirmish with me, but you'll lose the battle with women."

Jeff paced a lap through the room deep in thought, each kid watching intently as he went past them.

"Look, I don't care about the nuts and bolts of this thing. It sounds way too personal for my tastes. I'm just here to keep control of what happens inside this place while he's here."

"It's personal for me, too, you know?" she said, watching him pace back and forth. Maybe she was getting through to him. "This building is the home of my heritage. How can that not be personal? It was taken away from us once. I'm not about to let that happen again. Better believe me on that."

Jeff seemed to be softening on his stance. "I can tell it's important to you. But you need to understand that the Prince is here to stay, at least until he goes home."

"So you were hired to guard him and be his spokesperson?"

"I'm running his security, and if there are public announcements to be made, I'll make them. Mostly, he's letting his actions speak for themselves."

"Does anybody know he's even here?" Maile asked.

"There was an online press release last night."

Maile was beginning to piece things together. If the picketers outside had discovered the press release, they might've checked with her boss Thomas at Manoa Tours to see if Maile had a tour at the palace that day. With that information, they might've assumed she was a part of the Prince's plan to take over the palace as his own, and the protest organizer would've got the permit to picket. It was a stretch, but she'd had stranger things happen on tours since becoming a guide.

"May I have my bag?" asked.

"For?"

"Just my phone. Your gang has already searched us for weapons."

"Who do you want to call?"

Malice at the Palace

"Mrs. Abrams, the US federal prosecutor. I'd like to know if she still has plans on taking his case to trial, or if she's thinking of letting him go."

"You're friends with her?" he asked.

"Anything but. I do have her number stored in my phone."

"And if I don't let you call her?" Jeff asked.

"Forget about me being cooperative."

"Have you been yet?" he asked.

"More than you realize."

Chapter Seven

Jeff had Omar bring Maile's bag while he untied her wrists. They watched intently as she dug through to find her phone, while Omar's finger sat near the trigger of his gun. When she pulled her hand out, she was careful to display the phone to both of them. Scrolling for the number she wanted, even she could see her hands tremble with nerves.

"Mrs. Abrams, this is Maile Spencer. I'm sure you remember me?"

"Miss Spencer? Yes, of course. I'm a little busy right now. Maybe I can call you back later?"

"Actually, I'm busier than you are, and this is more important than whatever you have on your desk right now."

"What makes you think that?"

"Two men with guns are glaring at me right now. Guess where we are?"

"I don't know what you're talking about, Miss Spencer."

"I'm trapped, no, being held hostage by gunmen in the Iolani Palace along with nine kids on a tour. That's what I'm talking about."

"You need to hang up and call the police for something like that, not a lawyer. There's nothing I can do about men with guns."

"It has everything to do with you, Mrs. Abrams. These men are bodyguards in the employ of Prince Aziz, who has taken up residence here in the Iolani Palace. The reason I called was to ask just exactly why this is

Malice at the Palace

happening?" Maile did her best not to scream the last few words.

"I don't know anything about that. Now, if you please..."

"No, we're not playing a game of your hanging up on me, Mrs. Abrams. You've done that before. If you do it this time, whatever happens to me and those kids will be on your hands, and conscience, for the rest of your life."

"What do you want from me?"

"I need to know, right now, if you have plans on starting a new trial on Prince Aziz's case? And if not, when will he be able to leave Honolulu?"

"Neither of those answers are under my control."

"Why not? You're the federal District Attorney, and..."

"Federal Prosecutor."

"I don't care what your job title is. Don't you decide these things? You were the one who let him out on his own recognizance, right?"

"Let me assure you I had nothing to do with that. It was Judge Craven who declared a mistrial, and then granted the defense's request that Prince Aziz be let out."

"Mistrial? Isn't that where something goes wrong with evidence or testimony and the judge decides to start all over with a new trial?"

"Basically, yes. But why is Prince Aziz there? You said you're at the Iolani Palace?" Abrams asked.

"That's what has been my question for the last two hours. According to his bodyguards, this palace is the only place good enough for Aziz simply because it's a

69

royal palace, and he's planning to stay here until the government lets him go home."

"That's going to be quite a while, because his new trial won't start for several more weeks."

Maile had to calm herself. "Maybe you don't understand. Aziz has already moved into the King's Bedroom and is currently taking a nap on King Kalakaua's bed. He's not going anywhere until the federal government, the same federal government you work for Mrs. Abrams, allows him to go home to Khashraq. And he has half a dozen armed bodyguards here to protect him."

"Eight altogether," Jeff said to remind her.

"Eight, Mrs. Abrams, eight bodyguards are in the Iolani Palace, all armed with guns and wearing bulletproof vests. They're guarding entrances, hallways, even the restroom."

"I should contact the police SWAT team, and maybe the US Marshals. That's a matter for them manage, with force if necessary."

"No, actually, this is a diplomatic problem. First of all, I have a group of nine Australian teens here, and they're being held hostage just like I am, along with one of the docents. They've had nothing to eat or drink in several hours, and honestly, they're holding up great. I'm proud of them for doing so well. If the SWAT team burst in through doors, I hate the idea that these kids might get caught in the crossfire."

"I'm not a police officer, Miss Spencer. I don't know about things like crossfire."

Maile ignored her. "And something needs to be done before it gets leaked to the press. Each of these kids

Malice at the Palace

has parents waiting for them back at their hotels. Do you like the idea of making them worry for their children?"

"No, but…"

Again, Maile interrupted. "I hate the idea that violence might break out in the palace. I know that's unimportant to you, but it's of great importance to me as a citizen of Hawaii and as a Hawaiian. So, even you should be able to see how big of a diplomatic nightmare this already is, and the longer it goes, the worse it will become. That's on you, Mrs. Abrams, so don't try and pass the buck back to me."

Maile couldn't hear Abrams' reply when Jeff took the phone from her hand. "Who is this again?" he asked Maile.

"Federal prosecutor that's trying to put Aziz in prison for international sex crimes and human trafficking."

Jeff put the phone to his ear. "Mrs. Abrams, this is Jeff Bedford. I'm in charge of Prince Aziz's security while he's here at the palace. He has also asked me to be his spokesman when dealing with authorities and the media. He wants everyone to know…"

He was interrupted and listened for a moment.

"No, there are no specific ransom demands. Prince Aziz's only demand is that he is allowed to return to his own country."

Maile watched as Jeff listened for a moment.

"Yes, that's correct. He has no intention of going anywhere except to the airport for a flight on his personal aircraft to home. His family's private Gulfstream is already there."

More listening.

"No, he's quite adamant about not staying in a hotel. Only here at the palace."

Maile watched as Jeff's jaw muscles worked overtime.

"Look, I know nothing about his cousin or a nephew leaving on a plane the other day. That has nothing to do with this."

Jeff postured while listening. Maile noticed his trigger finger rubbing the smooth metal on the side of his weapon.

"Yes, we're all armed and willing to engage in combat with any threat from outside forces. Let me assure you and anyone thinking of launching a rescue of Miss Spencer or any of her tourists, or anyone considering the capture of Prince Aziz, that my team is willing to battle to the last man in the protection of the Prince." He jabbed his thumb on the *End Call* button and shoved the phone into Maile's chest. "She's a piece of work."

"Isn't she, though?" Maile said, while quickly checking for messages or texts. She returned texts to her brother and to Lopaka, who was apparently still waiting at the bus under the banyan trees next to the palace. She tried to be coy and slip the phone into a pocket, but it was grabbed from her hand by Omar. "She's what I have to deal with on the flip side of Prince Aziz. Maybe now you understand why I'm so unwilling to cooperate with this stupid scheme of yours."

"Not my scheme. It was given to me when I was hired."

"Make it stop, then."

"I can't, okay?"

"What did she tell you about the Prince's cousin?" Maile asked.

"It sounds like his father sent a body double on some sort of covert rescue mission for his son."

"But the Prince is still here," Maile said. "That doesn't make sense. Why did the double go home and leave the Prince here if it was a rescue mission?"

"I have no idea. None of this is making any sense right now," he said quietly.

"Who exactly is upstairs?" Maile asked.

Jeff sent Omar away before finally giving Maile his full attention. "The Prince. He was supposed to have gone home using the identity of the double. It was an elaborate plan that they worked on for weeks, to get the Prince home again. I don't know why he didn't go. All I know is that for as illogical and senseless as it is, I'm running this operation for the Aziz family. Now this Abrams woman has been brought into the mix, something no one ever planned on."

"And that's what I've been dealing with for several months. Just a bunch of screwball stuff that makes no sense whatsoever." The last kid returned from the restroom and took a chair with his friends. Maile took Jeff off to one side as far from the kids as she could. "Seriously, everything to do with that guy is like watching some old Three Stooges movie. Unfortunately, I'm the one getting boinked in the eye with a finger."

Jeff smiled for the first time. "Sorry you're a part of that."

"Are you guys going to kill us?"

He seemed surprised by her question. "We don't want to kill anyone, but we will defend the Prince, if it comes to that."

"Including you? I mean, you're American. What stakes do you have in this game?"

"I'm being paid to do this."

"And you're willing to kill others, kill the police or federal agents? Just for some money?"

He took Maile even further away. "Look, his kingdom isn't much to brag about. I doubt it's even as big as this island, but when we invaded there during the height of the Iraq War, they took a hit. Things were bad for a few days, with us and the few troops they had caught in the middle of a prolonged firefight with the Iraqis. The only thing that saved our butts were the Khashraqi people, opening their doors to American troops to feed and shelter us. Ever since then, our government has been promising to rebuild their country, but so far, not much has happened. The Aziz family runs just about every ministry of the country, and they've been getting the run-around from the US government ever since then. I was a part of that leading force that invaded their country, so yeah, I feel some obligation to them."

"Well, I'm very sorry about what happened in the war, but maybe you don't know this Aziz guy as well as I do."

"I've read every bio I could find, as well as US intel reports. He checks out as friendly to American interests."

"Friendly might be the right word, and a little too much."

Malice at the Palace

"What's with the human trafficking stuff?" he asked. "I never picked up on anything like that in reports about him."

"Of course not. It's illegal all over the world. He's certainly not going to advertise he's doing it."

"How do you know so much about it?"

"Because I was almost one of those women."

"That's why it's so personal? Why you're angry at him?"

"Every woman on the planet should be angry at him. But yeah, he came to Honolulu for a tour that I took him on. At the end of the day, he propositioned me with way too much money, and the promise of even more if I'd join him in his room that night. Just as I was telling him to take a hike, the police and the FBI showed up. The police took me in for prostitution, while the FBI dealt with Aziz. I've had legal trouble because of him ever since."

"Is that something you do on the side?" he asked.

"No! The police took me in just to get me away from him, without Aziz losing face in public. His MO, or whatever it's called, is to lure women into his hotel room, drug them, stick them on his private airplane, and go on to the next location. That was supposed to be LA, but he's been here in Honolulu ever since."

"How long ago was that?"

"Several months. That Abrams woman got involved as the lead federal prosecutor. I guess something got fouled up and a mistrial was declared, and now Aziz is out on his own recognizance." Maile shook her head. "I guess that means taking up residence here in the Iolani Palace until he's allowed to go home. And you, Mister

Bedford, are now officially one of the Stooges. Welcome to the show."

"That's not exactly the problem."

"It is to me. I still don't see why you're involved?"

"The reason I was hired is because I can speak Arabic to the bodyguards, and I'll be the English language spokesman with the media. The problem started when..."

"I'll tell you when the problem started," Maile said. "The problem started when Aziz invaded the building, bringing armed gunmen with him. Tell me, Jeff, how does a handyman go from putting locks on someone's door to becoming a hostage taker so easily?"

"There's much more to this situation than holding a few hostages, or getting the Prince safe passage home, Miss Spencer."

"That sounds like plenty to me. What else could there be?"

"The Prince has decided you will be his wife."

Chapter Eight

Maile was glad her hands were tied again, because she was ready to take a swing at someone.

"His what?"

"You might have a point about the Prince wanting women to take home in the past, but the trip he's currently on is for a wife, not concubines."

"There're no women in Khashraq willing to marry him?" she asked.

"Probably plenty, but none of royal birth. You see, there's only one royal family in his country, and all the females in that family in his generation are either too closely related or already married."

"What's that got to do with me?"

"The Prince hired a team of legal and genealogical experts, and they came up with a list of names of available women of royal birth. Your name's on the list."

"Mine? Why am I on that list?"

"You're of royal birth, right?"

"Well, yes, in a round-about and very minimal way. But it's Hawaiian royalty, something that hasn't really existed for a hundred years. What use am I to the Prince?"

"The way I understand it is that royalty is royalty to the Aziz family, especially when it comes to the prince."

"I don't know what that means," Maile said.

"It means beggars can't be choosers. Apparently, the prince has been around the world, dropping in on the royal families with daughters that are the right age."

"He hasn't had any takers, and now he's scraping the bottom of the barrel with me?" she asked.

Jeff looked away for a moment. "Pretty much."

"Well, now that isn't insulting at all."

"Maybe it's true, that in the past he's gone around the world a few times looking for women to take home, in one condition or another. But because of pressure from his father, he needs to find a wife and start a family. It would need to be a royal birth, and that requires a royal wedding to a woman of royal heritage. None of the remaining European families would even entertain him, and the Asian monarchies saw right through his scheme. That leaves you and some sort of Burmese princess, born and raised in LA and who denies her birthright to her throne, if that monarchy was ever reinstated. In fact, she does the counter-culture anarchy thing every chance she gets."

"Rage against the machine, even though she benefits from it?" she asked.

"Right. Just like your protesting friends outside."

"So, the Prince's last choice was between me and an anarchist? That's even more humiliating."

"It is what it is, Miss Spencer."

"Not much comfort in that motto."

"He wants you to know that if you were to marry him, you'd live a life of ease in his private quarters in the family palace. And if I figure it right, I doubt you'd see him very often."

"Only when he got tired of his concubines?"

"I'm supposed to tell you that living in Khashraq wouldn't be a bad life. His family is even willing to accept you the way you are."

Maile put her hands on her hips. "The way I am?"

"Divorced."

"Yes, divorced, as in used goods. Such a shame, that his family needs to settle for an impure woman of minimal royal heritage."

"Many women would consider doing it, only for the unimaginable wealth."

"Good for them. Except I'd have no freedom, and would only serve to be a baby factory for his family. I don't even know the family name."

"His full name is Mahmoud Naguib Aziz ibn Khashraq."

"There's the wedding of the year. Do you, Prince Pompous Mahmoud Naguib Aziz ibn Khashraq, take Kamali'i-wahine Hokuhoku'ikalani Spencer to be your awful wedded wife…"

Jeff snickered for a moment before stopping himself. "Be careful saying things like that. Khashraq is the name of the family and the name of the country."

"Of course." While pacing from one side of the large room to the other then back again, Maile tugged at the cord holding her wrists together. "Your problem is to convince me to go along quietly like a good little princess, while my problem is how to avoid being abducted to some sandbox where I'll be kept captive, only to provide favors for His Majesty, Prince Pervert of Khashraq. At least until I can no longer hide the wrinkles or have to put henna in my hair to cover the white ones. Sorry, not interested."

"He's hired me not just to run his security operations here in Hawaii, but to convince you of cooperating."

"Cooperating with you or him?"

"Both, if possible. It's to everyone's best interest that you do."

"Oh, really?" Maile had a hard time not shouting. "How is it in my best interest to be his wife?"

"You would prosper quite nicely. You were onto something a moment ago. He doesn't want you for the rest of your life. He simply wants a couple of children, one boy and one girl. Then you'd be able to quietly walk away with a divorce and a bank account, of course."

"Of course. And if I were able to produce a son first, that would be best, right?"

"That's how it generally works, yes."

"How much is his family willing to pay me to produce heirs to the throne before walking away in silence?"

"You could count on eight digits."

"For that, I'd have to put up with his creepy family, and give up my children forever?"

"It wouldn't be the first time this has been done."

"First time for me." She tugged at her bindings again. "But right now, my guests and I need something to eat. Have any contingency plans for that?"

"The Prince needs halal foods."

"I don't care about what he needs. I only care about getting some food into those kids before they mount a revolt of their own."

"I need to find someone that delivers halal. If they continue to behave themselves, I'll order enough for your guests, too."

"Halal in Honolulu?" Maile made no attempt to keep from laughing at him. "We're the crossroads of the

Malice at the Palace

Pacific, not of the Middle East. You might be able to find kosher food. Halal is pretty tough. What's he been eating these last few weeks?"

"He takes a butcher and chef everywhere with him. They do his food preparation. He has staff for pretty much everything."

"Are they here in the palace?"

"No. Just his security detail."

"Well, I don't know much about halal or kosher food, but you might have a tough time feeding your prince relying on food being delivered. In the meantime, what're you going to do about feeding the kids and me?"

"Isn't there a kitchen here? Seems like a royal palace should have one," he said.

"The only one that I know of is in the basement, a little convenience thing for employees to eat their lunches."

Jeff checked the time on his watch. "I need to go talk with the Prince."

"May we look for something to eat?" she asked before he got far.

"Help yourself. Just don't try and leave the building."

"Or what happens?"

"Australian teenagers and Hawaiian women look just like bad guys through MAC-10 iron sights. To answer your next question, I'm sending Omar and another guard with you, just to make sure none of you strays too far."

"May I please be untied?"

Jeff undid the knot in the cord around her wrists. "Just remember, this can go back on at any time, just like that blindfold, or a gag, if it came to that."

With two cranky guards acting as their chaperones, Maile took the kids down to the break room in the basement. Getting there, the fridge and cabinets were instantly raided of everything, including a couple of lunches that had been left behind be employees. Watching the kids negotiate who was getting what to eat, she started to piece things together.

Every employee and docent had already been let go except for Mrs. Goodwin. Guards were now posted at each exit to keep anyone else from leaving. The Prince wasn't going anywhere until his demands were met, and that was for him and Maile to be granted safe passage to his plane at the airport, something told to Mrs. Abrams on a second call to her. Mrs. Goodwin and the school kids were simply pawns in the game that was being played between Maile, the Prince, his spokesman and guards, and a federal prosecutor.

"Some tour guide I've turned out to be," she mumbled, rubbing her wrists where the cord had been removed.

Maile watched as Omar had a quick conversation with the other guard and left him at the doorway. She'd heard a couple of the Prince's bodyguards use English, and she wondered how much Jeff had been lying to her about them not knowing the language well. Something stunk about what was going on in the palace that day, that there was much more to it than met the eye. She just couldn't figure out what it was.

Malice at the Palace

"Miss Spencer, we need to call our parents," Margo said. She'd found instant oatmeal to cook in the microwave. All of them had found something but one girl, who seemed reluctant to eat.

"I know. They must be terribly worried. I tried to keep my phone, but it was taken away from me again." She looked behind her at the guard at the door and lowered her voice. "Do any of you have a phone?"

"I do!" Trevor said. He began to reach into a pocket. "It's an old flip phone. They didn't find it on me."

"Just relax, Trevor," Maile said. She had to keep her voice casual, as if they were simply having a conversation, and hoped that their one guard couldn't understand what was being said. "Leave it in your pocket until later. Can you make local Honolulu calls with it?"

"Oh yes. They're longies, back to Oz, and then bounced back to here. Terribly expensive. Mum would have a fit if she knew I was making long distance local calls."

"We might need to set aside worrying about your mom being upset about the call. I'm glad to pay her back later." Maile wondered how trustworthy the kids were, if they'd go along with whatever she asked them to do. "You know what? Maybe you should give me the phone?" She watched carefully, and just as his hand holding the phone rose above the level of the table, she waved for him to lower it. "Just pass it along from one person to the next under the table."

The kids along one side of the long table sat frozen to their chairs, their hands hidden beneath the table, elbows moving back and forth. When the phone got to Irene, the youngest in the group, it was dropped, hitting the floor with a clatter. Their guard at the door must've heard the noise also. When he looked back at them, Irene was just sitting up again. Maile could tell she was close to tears.

"What is it?" the guard demanded in broken English.

Margo took over when she held something up. "Dropped me spoon. Sorry."

When he went back to leaning against the doorjamb, the kids returned to passing along the phone, now at lightning speed. Once Maile had it, she slipped it under her skirt and snagged it over the band of her undies with the hope it would be hidden by the pleats in her skirt. All she hoped for was that the battery was still good and that she could remember how to send text messages on a flip phone. She also needed to remember a couple of numbers, and hoped they would reply, even though they wouldn't recognize the sender.

"Miss Spencer, I don't think those guys are going to let us go home tonight," Margo said, once her oatmeal was done.

"I think you're right. That's why I need Trevor's phone, to call someone for some help."

"Evie needs to go back to the hotel."

"All of you do. I'm trying to figure out a plan for that," Maile said. "You'll have to find something to eat, Evie. It might be a while before any of us get a real meal."

"I need me insulin before I can eat."

That got Maile's full attention. "You need what?"

Now Evie was close to tears. "Insulin. It's in the fridgy back at the hotel. I was supposed to be back to the room by now."

Maile went to where the girl sat at the end of the table. "How much do you take every day?"

"Just once in the morning, but I have to check my blood sugar before I eat, and take more insulin if it's high."

"And that's why you're not eating," Maile said. "You didn't bring your monitor with you?"

Evie shook her head.

"How are you feeling?"

"Okay, so far. Getting hungry, though."

As a nurse, Maile knew hunger and diabetes didn't go well together. Feeding the kid a meal without insulin wouldn't do much good, and might cause more harm. But if she waited too long, Evie could suffer the consequences of extreme low blood sugar, and become unconscious. Dealing with Jeff was her best course of action in getting Evie to a hospital, or at least getting some insulin delivered.

"I'll try to figure out something. I might be able to get us out before you have problems."

"But that man said no one is leaving," Margo said.

"I'm trying to think of an escape plan."

"Oh, wow!" one of the Hacky Sack Kids said. He hushed when he was elbowed by the girl next to him. Then he whispered, "Count me in!"

"What's your name?" Maile asked.

"They call me Bongo, like the drums."

"Okay, Bongo, I'll need a big, strong guy like you to help the younger kids."

Bongo was smiling. "Are we going to rush the door?"

"Um, no. Best to get that idea out of your head right now. Those guys are serious about using their guns. Let's not do anything stupid that makes them mad, okay?"

"Fine with me," Margo said.

"What can we do?" Irene asked. It was amazing how one kid could be so close to tears for so long and never start crying.

"You guys said your hometown is famous for caves? Have any of you gone through those caves?"

"Irene's your girl for that," Margo said.

"You like going in caves and tunnels?"

Irene nodded. "Go with me dad all the time. I can fit in the tight spots he has trouble with."

"How would you like to be the first person to get out of here?"

Irene's face seemed to brighten at the thought. "Please?"

"You and Evie will be at the front of the line."

Maile ate whatever was leftover from the kids eating their meals. That was the end crust of a loaf of bread, leftover rice that would've been tossed out at home, and an orange she shared with her new partner in deception, Irene.

"When are we cracking out of here?" Bongo asked.

"We're not cracking out. Okay, maybe we are, but not for a while. I still need to make one more friend. You kids wait in here." Maile got up from her chair, hoping to use the bathroom. "And for goodness sakes, don't do anything stupid like running for the doors. Those are real guns with real bullets, not pretend stuff like in the movies."

Pantomiming most of her message with the guard at the door, Maile negotiated a trip to the restroom, the next room over from the kitchen. There was no lock on the door, and she knew another bodyguard had positioned himself just outside. As soon as she was in, she searched for any way out. There were no windows and the ventilation grates were too small for a person to squeeze through, just four walls and the necessary plumbing fixtures. She'd been hoping for a window, since the lowest floor was only partially subterranean. It would've been an easy drop out the window and a short run to where she hoped Lopaka was still waiting with the van. No such luck with an escape route, though.

Sitting on her own porcelain throne, she sent a text to Lopaka's phone using the secret flip phone from one of the kids.

Borrowed phone. Where RU? Maile

A moment later a return text came: *They kept me out at gunpoint. Sorry!*

Police know we're here?

Called Ota. He's getting SWAT.

No! No SWAT!

??

Too dangerous.

Call him direct, was Lopaka's last message.

Maile tried remembering Detective Ota's phone number. It took three mis-sent texts before she got him.

Getting SWAT prepped.

No! 8 gunmen!

What kind of guns? Ota asked.

IDK. Bigger than pistols, smaller than machine guns. They're wearing BP vests. Serious stuff.

How many hostages?

Me + nine kids + one docent.

Where? he asked.

Me + kids in basement level, kitchen. IDK docent. Haven't seen her in a while.

Anyone else?

The Prince in the King's room.

Keep everyone together in kitchen.

I need insulin.

?

One kid is diabetic. She needs insulin. And a monitor.

I'm sending SWAT and paramedics.

No! Maile wasn't going to listen to someone outside. It was her group to watch over. She also didn't want gunplay in the palace. *I have plan. I think.*

Don't risk something dumb. Let me handle.

Get me that insulin and wait two hours. Then you can send SWAT. More later.

When Maile didn't get a return message, she hoped he had listened and would back off with the SWAT team.

Maile didn't know the building as well as the docents, but had done enough term papers on the palace as a kid to know there was one set of stairs from the main floor to the basement. The entrances to the building were on the main floor, the only way in or out of the building except to jump from an upper floor window. That would result in a hard landing on either asphalt or lawn grass, risking broken bones. A broken leg, or just a twisted ankle, wouldn't allow a quick getaway. Jumping out a window wasn't any better than risking getting caught in crossfire from Ota's SWAT team.

Try as she might, Maile couldn't remember where it was that she'd read about a secret passageway from the main floor to the outside. Legend had it that Queen Lili'uokalani would sneak out late at night to visit with friends in dark corners of the grounds during her imprisonment. If that were true, Maile might be able to get the kids out the same way. But it was a legend, and like so many tales told in the islands, it wasn't very reliable.

Fuzzy memory made her believe the imaginary tunnel led to the Coronation Pavilion, a couple hundred feet from the front entrance and off to one side. But that had been built more than a century before, and trees had grown to maturity in that time. If there really was a tunnel, it could be filled with roots looking for water, or it could've collapsed in decades gone by. Just the idea of crawling through a dark tunnel filled with spiders and rats gave her a shudder.

"Not much choice," she muttered. She got the phone to send another test to Lopaka.

Go to Manoa House. Get Mom. Look for tunnel out of palace. Maybe to Coro Pav?

Escape route? he asked in return.

Right. Hurry.

On it!

At least she had help on the outside. She might've been sending Lopaka on a wild goose chase looking for a book of secrets in the Manoa House library, but having someone outside helping gave her some reassurance.

Don't tell Mom there's trouble!!! she texted.

"I still need insulin," she whispered.

There was one thing she could do, and that would require asking a friend at the hospital to break a few rules. She had a text conversation with one of her old workmates about what she needed.

One vial of reg insulin, syringe, and a monitor. Can you do it? she asked.

Dinner break in half hour. Why are we texting? Daniel asked by text. He was a male nurse in the ER at Honolulu Med that owed her a favor.

Don't worry about that. Just put the stuff on the front porch of the palace and leave. Repeat. Don't hang around. Leave.

Maile sighed with relief when she got a return text that he'd comply. All she could do now was wait.

Malice at the Palace

Chapter Nine

Maile knew she'd been in the bathroom for too long. She had one last thing to do. Closing her eyes, she relaxed and mumbled quietly. Jolting her out of her prayers was the banging of a fist on the door. "Mahlah! Khalas!"

Maile didn't know what he was saying, but figured he wanted her to wrap it up. Putting the phone back under her skirt in its hiding place, she left the restroom behind.

Jeff was standing there with the guard when she went out.

"Oh, hello. How's Aziz?" she asked, trying to sound nonchalant.

The guard threw a fit. "His name Prince Aziz!"

"Not in this building, he's not."

The guard raised his weapon as though he were going to use it to give her a solid whack in the head. Jeff said something in Arabic, a command of some sort, and pulled Maile away.

"Hey, don't antagonize these guys. You're dead meat to them, someone in their way, an obstacle."

"I thought I was supposed to be their next princess?"

"Right now, you're simply a pain in the neck," he said.

"Sorry to be so much trouble. Why not just show me and the kids the door?"

"Not gonna happen and don't even think of asking the Prince for that."

"So, what then? We're just going to hang out doing nothing while Aziz has a good night of sleep in the king's bed?"

"I've just communicated his demands to the mayor. Now, we have to wait until we hear back," Jeff said.

"The mayor? Why aren't you dealing with the federal government?"

"That's the highest ranking politician that would answer my call. Apparently, that Abrams woman has already called around, telling everybody there's a prank being played."

"That..." Maile bit her tongue, wondering if she should mention the police were mounting a SWAT team invasion, if it would change plans being made inside the palace. "You realize talking to the mayor is going to bring police and the media here, right?"

"That's what the Prince is hoping for. He figures the more attention he can bring to this, the sooner it'll be resolved."

"That's what we all want. What are his demands? Am I allowed to know, since I seem to be at the center of all this?"

"He wants safe passage to his Gulfstream at the airport, along with exoneration from all charges filed by the federal government."

Maile shrugged. "Okay with me. I'll hold the door open for him. I might even wave goodbye."

"No waving needed. You're going with him."

"Should've figured as much. What about the kids that are stuck with this mess?"

"As soon as I get the word that wheels are up, I let the kids go back to mommy and daddy."

"And what about you? The Prin...Aziz is leaving you behind?"

"I have something planned. I've already been paid, and my job will be done by then. Believe me, Miss Spencer, I have as much interest in going to Khashraq as you do."

"Speaking of the kids, one of them needs insulin. If she doesn't get it pretty soon, she could go into a diabetic coma or have seizures."

He patted himself down. "Didn't bring any."

It was time to fess-up. "I have some coming from the hospital, along with a blood sugar monitor. It should be delivered to the front door any time now."

Jeff tilted his head back and looked down his nose at her. "Just exactly how did they know to send some?"

Maile tried feigning innocence by shrugging. "Maybe they got a message?"

He looked her up and down for a moment, acting as though he might frisk her again. "Whatever's going on, don't let those idiots find out about it."

One of the guards showed up carrying a Honolulu Medical Center lunch bag. He and Jeff spoke in Arabic for a moment while they checked inside, until the bag changed hands and the guard returned to his post.

Jeff handed the precious cargo to Maile. "You owe me, big."

"Thanks," Maile said. She kept her captor out in the hall where the kids couldn't hear them talk. What she needed to do was plant the idea in his mind that she and the kids were planning on spending the night in the palace. "Is there any way we can get real food delivered? Maybe some blankets and pillows for them?"

"I'm bringing in his chef in the morning, with enough food for all of us for three days. Forget about being comfy."

"Three days? These kids won't last that long. A couple of them are close to losing it already, and it's not even ten o'clock. One of them said something about bedtime coming up pretty soon, and I know I saw a couple of them hiding yawns. There's nowhere for them to sleep, except on the floor. We can't stay here for three days."

"I'm trying to think of a way of getting some of them out of here," Jeff said quietly. "That might happen tomorrow morning when the chef shows up. If he's bringing large carts or tubs, I might be able to sneak the smaller kids out in those."

Maile couldn't wait that long, not with a diabetic kid, and others needing their parents. Plus, those parents would be freaking out by now. "Why not just let us go? Seriously, get the rest of the guards distracted with something, open the back door, and we'll run for it." Maybe he still didn't know the police were hiding nearby, and she still wasn't telling him that. If there was to be a teenaged jailbreak for freedom, hopefully the cops would see the kids and grab them before they got lost. Or shot at by overly protective guards. "There're trees back there to hide in once we're outside. Then all we have to do is climb the fence and bolt for the capitol building."

"Except these guys are too well-trained to get distracted so easily. They won't give up their posts."

"Okay, how about this? I make a rope ladder from some sheets and we climb out a window?"

"I've already checked the alarm system. All the windows are alarmed. What makes you think I'm going to help you, anyway?" Jeff asked.

"You just said you were trying to get some of us out." She held up the insulin kit. "And you let me have this."

"I'll help only if it means I don't get shot in the process. And don't think for a minute you're going anywhere. I get bonus pay if you're delivered to his Gulfstream, safe and sound."

"I thought you were American, one of the good guys?" she asked.

"Cut me some slack, will you? I'm in a tough spot. I need to keep that jerk upstairs happy, while trying to figure a way out for those kids."

"Does that mean you're starting to believe me about Aziz?" Maile asked.

"I made a couple of calls. What you told me checks out as okay."

"Not so princely, is he?"

Jeff looked at the ceiling as though he could see through to where Aziz was. "Maybe you should go use your kit before my patience is tested a little too much."

Omar had one hand resting on his weapon when he walked over to them. "What you talking about? You two stop talking!"

Jeff nudged Maile away, getting between her and Omar. The two men had a heated exchange of words in Arabic, before Omar wandered off again.

"What was that all about?" Maile asked, as Jeff steered her into the kitchen.

"Nothing for you to worry about."

"I've already got a lot to worry about, and a lot of it involves that guy's itchy trigger finger and his gun. What'd he say to you?"

"He and the other guards are getting hungry. They either want food brought in or want to go out to find something."

"Dressed the way they are and with weapons? They won't get far. Anyway, there's nothing open around her at this time of night."

"There's nothing nearby? This is downtown, isn't it?" Jeff asked.

"Downtown, but there's not much nightlife. They'd have to go to Chinatown to find a bar, and I can guarantee you that ain't gonna be halal, or whatever these guys eat."

"Is there delivery?"

"Pizza, but I doubt they'd deliver here to the Palace. They'd think it was a prank. I think your guys are outta luck, unless they want instant oatmeal."

Drawing their attention to the doorway were two voices arguing in Arabic. While Maile could only guess what it was about, Jeff listened intently. When a third voice joined the debate, Jeff sent Maile into the kitchen.

The kids made space at the table so Maile could work with Evie.

"You got that for me?" the girl asked.

"Yep, special delivery, just for you. First, I need to check your blood sugar."

"I can do it myself," the girl said quietly. Maile watched as she deftly sorted through everything she needed, pricked her finger for a drop of blood, and ran the test in the monitor.

"You're really good at that, Evie."

"I've been doing it for almost a year. Me mum always watches me, just like you are." The results came up on the monitor. "I should get five units of insulin, and then eat four hundred calories. Half of that should be complex carbohydrates, and some protein."

Maile set Margo to the task of making more instant oatmeal, and a hard-boiled egg was found for Evie's meal. "Does your mother give your insulin?"

"I'm still too chicken." Evie looked up with big eyes. "You said you're a nurse. Can you give it to me?"

"Be glad to. Only if you promise to help me later?"

After getting a nod from the girl, Maile gave the simple injection. Once the kit was put away, she watched as Evie started her meal. At least that problem was solved.

The other kids drew up chairs and encouraged their friend, bringing her milk. That gave Maile the chance to covertly check the flip phone for text messages from Lopaka. There weren't any. Instead of sending a text to him, she hid behind the door that was propped open and called.

"Brah, you're killing me making me wait so long," she whispered. She watched the kids still seated at the table as they watched her in return. "Find anything that can help us get out of here?"

"What's going on there now?"

"These knuckleheads are starting to argue with each other, and a few of them have itchy trigger fingers. The last I heard, Aziz is upstairs in the King's bedroom. Me and the kids are in the kitchen sharing a vial of insulin, which I would gladly trade for a bottle of wine. Did you or Mom find anything about tunnels?"

"She remembered something, but she's really pissed at you."

"You told her what happened?"

"She saw it on the news. It's even gone national."

Maile griped to herself for a moment. "At least it's the middle of the night. Maybe no one will notice me making a fool of myself. Or of Manoa Tours."

"Manoa Tours is getting great exposure, Mai."

She turned away, hoping the kids wouldn't hear her. "That's the last thing I need right now. What did my mom remember?"

Lopaka put Maile's mother, Kealoha, on the line.

"The Coronation Pavilion was originally built right in front of the main entrance, attached by a little bridge. After Kalakaua and Kapiolani's coronation, the pavilion was moved to where it is now."

"I know all that, Mom." Maile peeked through the gap between the door and the doorframe to see what the gunmen were doing. A fourth had joined the others in arguing with each other, and it looked like playground pushing and shoving would start soon. "What I need to know is if there are tunnels that lead away from the Palace?"

"Someone must've been thinking ahead when they moved it," Kealoha said slowly. "They dug two tunnels. The first one started to fill with water, so they dug another."

A fifth gunman showed up, also posturing. This one had his hand on his gun, his finger rubbing the side of it nervously. They all seemed to have problems with Jeff.

Malice at the Palace

Even if the tunnel led nowhere, Maile wondered if she might be able to hide the kids in there, and then tell a lie to the gunmen that they had escaped by a rope ladder out a window or off a balcony. She'd have to find a way of doing some staging for that with knotted bed sheets, though. "Mom, a little short on time here. Can you tell me where to find the access to the tunnels?"

"The second tunnel goes to the pavilion. It took almost a year to dig in secret, but they finished it. That's the story I heard a long time ago."

"It didn't fill with seawater?" Maile asked.

"How should I know? I don't go in tunnels."

The gunmen's voices got loud, and Jeff tried shouting them down.

"How do I find the entrance to the tunnel?" Maile whispered.

"It's under the pavilion."

"Mom!" Maile clenched her eyes, trying not to let her emotions burst. "Where's the other end of the tunnel? The entrance at the palace end?"

"You don't know? You're a tour girl and you don't know your way around the Iolani Palace?"

"Mom, please…"

"In the Throne Room. There's the door behind the thrones. That goes to stairs to the second floor bedrooms. Nobody ever used it. Queen Lili'uokalani preferred to use the same entrance as everyone else, and meet them informally."

"Less history, more current events. I've never been behind that door. Is there another set of stairs that go down?"

"Nobody else has ever been back there since Lili'uokalani, except maintenance people. They'd be closely supervised..."

"Stairs! Are there stairs?"

"I've never been behind that door, either."

Maile heard more commotion out in the hallway. When she peeked, she saw Jeff body slam Omar to the floor and hold him there.

Maile took a deep breath. "What's behind the door? Please, I'm begging you, just tell me how to find the tunnel entrance."

"I heard there's a trap door in the floor with a rug over it. It might be one of those fancy silk things from the Orient. If it is, you'll have to..."

"Yeah, sounds good. Put Lopaka back on."

"Maile girl, if you're going to give tours of the Palace, you should brush up on the history..."

"Lopaka!" When he finally came on, she exhaled. "Brah, things here are going downhill in a hurry. Were you able to find a schematic of the building? Anything that shows a tunnel going from beneath the Throne Room to the Pavilion?"

"I found something, but can you receive data?"

"Not on this crappy thing. Snap a pic of it and text it."

Maile ended the call and waited. Five minutes passed like hours before the picture arrived. She had some fiddling to do with the phone to move the blueprint image around, and it got fuzzy when she tried to enlarge it. There were too many lines to see one thing from another on the tiny screen. Noticing the battery bars blinking at her about the phone needing recharging, she turned the phone off and tucked it away beneath her skirt. Now all she had to do was find a way of getting the kids from the kitchen to the Throne Room without being seen by the angry gunmen who were now pushing and shoving each other for no apparent reason.

Feeling forced into a corner, Maile was putting all her hopes of escape on finding an unlocked trap door beneath a silk rug, being able to open it, and convincing nine teenagers it was a good idea to go into a tunnel that hadn't been used in possibly a century, if ever. To do that, she'd need to…

Her thoughts were interrupted by a gunshot.

Maile didn't bother peeking through the gap in the door. Instead, she looked out and saw Jeff on the floor, the other men standing around him looking bewildered. Omar was gesticulating at another man in Arabic while Jeff groped at his groin.

Maile's ER nurse training kicked in again. She grabbed towels from the kitchen counter.

"Okay, there's a big problem out there."

"Someone go shot, huh?" Margo asked.

"Yeah, I'm afraid so. When I go out there, you guys have to stay in here. Close and block the door with one of the tables. Make it as heavy as you can, and then stand off to the sides of the room, okay?"

"In case someone shoots through the door?" Bongo asked. He almost looked as though he were enjoying the moment.

There was more shouting in the hallway, some of which sounded like argument, some sounding like concern for Jeff.

"That's the idea. Can you do that for me?"

"Miss Spencer, how will you get back in here?" Margo asked.

"Don't worry about that. And don't open the door for anyone unless it's the police." Maile gave the idea some thought. "Make the police say their names. If one of them is named Ota, it's okay. Let him in."

Maile took a deep breath and stepped out in the hall.

Chapter Ten

Four men stood over Jeff. When Maile heard the kitchen door slam shut and noise inside like furniture being moved, she put the kids out of her mind. Holding the towels in one hand, she raised her hands and walked toward Jeff slowly.

"Is he shot?"

"He is bleed," Omar said. He looked as though he needed a cigarette break.

With her hands up, Maile took another step. "I'm just going to help him."

Omar postured and stepped back. The others moved back with him.

Jeff looked over the top of his head at her. He was in obvious pain. "Need a medic, not a tour guide. Nothing you can do for me."

Maile knelt next to him. Blood was coming from his groin, but at least it wasn't pulsatile. She immediately went to work at pressing towels on the wound, the same as she would've done with gauze in the Emergency Room in the past. "You'd be surprised at what I can do."

"Not afraid of the blood?" Jeff asked.

"Been here, done this, as they say. I was an ER nurse before becoming a tour guide. I can't do much more for you than this. Sorry."

"More than what those idiots did for me."

Omar stepped forward. "You call us idiots?"

"Yeah, you and Ahmed. Why don't the two of you go check on the Prince?"

After a moment of posturing, and Jeff aiming his gun at them, Omar led Ahmed away, going upstairs to the main level. That left three more gunmen to get rid of.

"You need to get to the hospital. We should call for an ambulance."

"No ambulance," one of the gunmen said. He was the one that had been fondling his gun with a finger.

"These idiots aren't going to trust an ambulance crew to come in here," Jeff said. "Is it all that bad?"

She'd already groped beneath him for an exit wound. "No exit wound. Are these guns small caliber?"

"This style is nine millimeter, same size as used in pistols."

"That's not so bad as those big military bullets you guys use." She reinforced her pad with another towel. "It's not pulsatile and I can control the bleeding with pressure. I don't get why you're not complaining more."

"Believe me, I'm doing my best to hold my tongue. You seem like a nice lady."

"I appreciate it. Okay, I can't sit here and babysit this thing all night. What I'm going to do is wad up one towel and then tie the others together to wrap around your leg, holding the wad in place. Are you going to be able to walk after that?"

"Not walking this off."

Maile finished with her simple bandage, and when she cinched it as tight as she could, she finally got a groan out of him. "I hope that hurt as much as I meant it to."

"I've met nicer nurses than you."

"Maybe that's why I was fired?" She helped him up and let him lean on her as they went toward the kitchen.

"I was thinking of a way of getting you and the kids out of here," he whispered as they went past one of the gunmen.

"Forget it. I already have something in the works."

"I don't see how."

"How do I know I can trust you?" she asked.

"Now that I've been shot by one of them, I'm fully on your side. I just have to keep up the façade that I'm in charge. What's your idea?"

"Your friends aren't very good at frisking people. One of the kids still had an old-fashioned flip phone, and I've been using that to make calls and send texts. Sorry."

"An hour ago, that would've got you in a lot of trouble. Who've you been talking to? Cops?"

"Them, and someone doing some research for me."

"Sending in SWAT? Because those idiots aren't afraid to return fire, and they each have a couple hundred rounds of ammo each."

They got to the kitchen door and Maile tried pushing in. When the door wouldn't budge, she banged her hand on the door.

"Who is it?" one of the kids said through the door. It might've been Margo.

"Maile. Open up."

"How do we know it's Maile?" a boy asked.

"Have you seen any other women in the building tonight?" she hollered at the door. When noise of furniture came through the door, she put her attention back on Jeff, who was leaning more weight on her now. "I'm still not sold I can trust you."

"You can trust me as much as I'm trusting you right now."

There was the sound of more scraping of something heavy on the floor inside the kitchen.

"Can these guys understand English?" Maile asked, nodding her head at the men standing a little too close for comfort.

"Not these. What's your plan?" Jeff asked.

"I have a detective, a friend of sorts, waiting outside. He's giving me until just a little after midnight before he sends in the SWAT team."

"Let him, if that's the plan. I won't get in their way."

"That's not the plan." The kids finally got the door open and Maile helped Jeff inside. Once they were in, she could see the boys armed with brooms and a dish scrubber, and the girls had butter knives in their hands. "I need to make a call and send a couple of texts before I know if my idea will work. But it'll require a lot of cooperation from everybody, including you, Jeff."

Once he was plunked down in a chair, some of the kids gathered around to see his bloody bandage while others backed away. A chair was put in front of him to prop up his legs. Irene seemed most interested. He dug his smart phone from a pocket and offered it to Maile.

"You know what? I'll stick to using the flip phone. People are expecting to see that caller number from me. It might be best if you stay as uninvolved as possible."

She had Jeff send the last two guards away to check exits. That gave her time to call Ota, still waiting outside somewhere.

"What's going on?" he demanded. "You were supposed to call half an hour ago."

"Ran into a little trouble."

"Who was it that came to the front door a while ago?"

"The hospital delivered some insulin. I'll need an ambulance in a few minutes."

"What happened? Are you okay?"

"I'm fine," Maile said, not really believing it. "One of the, well, men was shot by another. He can wait a few more minutes."

"I have a hostage negotiator here. Give the phone to whoever is in charge."

"I think that's me, actually. I have a plan…"

"Forget your plan!" Ota said. "I don't believe for one moment you're in charge in there. I'm sending in SWAT."

"Just hear me out. I can save a lot of bloodshed and desecration of this place if everybody cooperates with me."

"What is it, then?" Ota asked.

"When I tell you to, I want you to call the security alarm company and have them set off the alarms."

"You mean turn them off?" Ota asked.

"No, set them off so they're alarming. Every alarm in the building. The name of the company is All-Island Alarms. Then contact Island Fire Equipment. They're the ones who monitor the fire alarm system here. Have them set off the building alarms at the same time as the security alarms, but without setting off the sprinklers."

"How do you know who runs the alarm systems?"

"Stickers with company logos on emergency exits. Five minutes after those alarms go off, I'm shutting down the electricity in the entire building."

"You're hoping the confusion buys you some time to rush a back door?" he asked. "That never works, Maile."

To speak with Ota privately, she walked away from Jeff, who'd been listening. "We're not going to rush the back door. My mother told me about a trapdoor in the Throne Room that leads to a tunnel."

"How'd you talk to your mother?"

"I called Lopaka. He's spent the evening with her."

"Is there anyone you haven't called since becoming a hostage?"

"Stay with me, okay? My problem is that I don't know if the tunnel is open. If it is, it would lead us to the Coronation Pavilion. Then my next problem would be getting out of that."

"Hold on a second," he said. She listened as he borrowed a laptop the SWAT team had. "Okay, I'm checking images online of the pavilion. It looks like there's some sort of hatch on the side of the steps that go up to it. You might be able to force that open."

"I'm not breaking up historical buildings, Detective. I'm not a rock star."

"You will if you want to get away. I might be able to send someone early to get that hatch open."

"Forget it. Don't bring any attention to it. Just have some cars parked nearby for the kids."

"They can park opposite the banyans, but they'll have the fence to deal with."

"I have an idea," she said, wondering how crazy it would sound. She didn't share it yet. "What do you think of my plan?"

"Not much. I see a lot of things going wrong."

"And I see a lot of people getting shot in a building that has suffered enough trouble at the hands of non-Hawaiians. One man has already been shot. I'm not allowing it to happen again."

"Maile, the only reason you're winning this argument is because you're more stubborn than I am. What time do you want the alarm shutdown?"

"It's a quarter to twelve now. Make it for ten after. Five minutes after that, the lights will go out. Hopefully. It'll take another five to ten minutes to get to the tunnel, and if everything goes right, we'll be at the pavilion a few minutes after that." She almost laughed at her own timeline. "Not exactly a rocket ship launch sequence, is it?"

"To use one of your favorite words, it's just nutty enough to work. But as soon as I see the lights go out, you have five minutes to get out before I send in SWAT." Ota gave commands to someone at his end of the call. "What happens if the tunnel isn't passable?"

"I have no idea. Hide in the tunnel, I guess. Just don't forget us in there."

It had taken several hours to convince Jeff to help her, and she still wasn't done. She went back to Jeff and reinforced his dressing with a dry bar towel. With a glance at the door, she saw two gunmen now holding it open so the kids couldn't block it closed. "Okay, look. I need your help," she whispered.

"Not giving up my weapon."

"I'm not asking you to. That thing is your problem, not mine. But I will tell you that if anyone else gets hurt by one of those things, I'll do my best to make sure someone goes to prison for it."

"What do you want me to do?" he asked.

Maile explained about the alarm systems going off at any minute. "I need you to somehow get to the fuse box and shut down the electricity to the building all at once. Can you do that?"

"Where is it?"

"There are two fuse boxes. I don't know what the difference is between them. There's a janitor's closet between the two restrooms down the hall. They're in there."

"Then what happens?" Jeff asked.

Maile gave the rest of her plan some thought, if she really trusted him enough to be specific. "Me and the kids run for the front door of the building and race for the street out front."

He shook his head. "They're guarding every exit. You won't get close, even in the dark."

"Don't worry about us. We'll be fine. Once it's dark, you can do whatever you want. I suggest you hit the rear exit and get as far from the building as you can." Maile was suggesting that because she knew Ota and SWAT were in that general direction, and would have an ambulance nearby. She needed to send Jeff in their direction if he were to get prompt medical assistance for his gunshot wound. "I also suggest you get rid of the gun once you're outside. You'll last longer."

One of the gunmen walked over and had a word with Jeff. At the end, he gave Maile a glare.

"What did he have to say?" Maile asked.

"He doesn't like Hawaii."

"I doubt I'd like Khashraq, and you can tell him that."

Malice at the Palace

"He also said Hawaiians are soft."

"Too bad for us. Are you okay? Having much pain?" she asked him.

"Don't worry about me," he said. He removed the magazine and checked the ammo before ramming it back in the gun again. "I'll find a way out of my own."

She looked at the gun that was still attached to his bulletproof vest. "How do you take that thing off, anyway?"

"It's just a simple clip," he said, demonstrating once. "Don't try and take these off someone, because they can shoot you even while it's still attached."

"Like I said, I'm not going to shoot anyone."

Maile took the flip phone and hid in a corner so she could send more text messages. The first was to Ota.

Sirens at 12:10? she asked.

Set and ready to go.

We're going at 12:15. Meet us at the pav at 12:30.

"How're you getting past the guards in the hallway?" Jeff asked. "I've sent the others on a patrol of the building and to guard the Prince, but there're still two in the hallway to make sure you and the kids don't try something. Which you are."

"I won't worry about you getting out, and you don't need to worry about those guards. They'll be dealt with."

"You aren't thinking of attacking them with brooms, are you?" Jeff asked.

Maile looked at the boys still holding brooms, and girls with butter knives. "Kids, put those things away. You need to be ready to go."

"To where, Miss Spencer?" Margo asked.

"You'll see. But it's going to be dark, and we'll all have to be as quiet as we can."

Just then, security alarms began to blare throughout the building, their echoes off walls making it sound like twice as many. The kids looked nervous, but Maile waved for them to be quiet. A few seconds later, the fire alarms also began to blare, creating twice as much noise.

"Are we okay, Miss Spencer?" Margo asked.

Maile held her finger to her lips in a silent request for them to be quiet. She went to the wall next to the kitchen counter, pulled the fire extinguisher from its bracket, and went out into the hall.

Both gunmen were there, scanning the walls and ceiling for the alarms, talking to each other while their hands were fiddling nervously with their weapons. Maile had to sell her next part as best as she could.

"Oh no!" she shouted, pointing at the ceiling with one hand while clinging to the extinguisher in the other. "Fire! Fire upstairs!"

The two gunmen looked at each and shared a quick message before one ran off to the stairs. That left one guard to deal with. He began pacing back and forth in front of the kitchen door. Just as he was about to ask Jeff a question, Maile got to him.

"Hey! Do you know how this thing works?" she asked the gunman of the extinguisher.

He looked. Pointing at something, he said something in Arabic.

"Like this?" Maile swung the cone blower attachment out and tried squeezing the grip. Nothing happened.

He said something while pulling a pin from the handle.

"Oh, I see. It works like this?"

This time, she aimed the extinguisher directly in the gunman's face and let him have it with a long squeeze. When he stumbled backwards swinging his arms, she followed, continuing to spray his face, coating him with a heavy layer of white powder. When the gunman bumped into the wall behind him, it knocked him back to his senses. Just as he was grabbing for his gun, Maile's fire extinguisher began to weaken. Hearing Jeff's words about how a gunman only had to swing the gun up to fire it, it gave her the answer of what to do next. Swinging the canister up as fast as she could, she caught him under the chin. She expected a clunk, and got a clank sound instead, along with the clack of his teeth hitting together. When his head went back, she saw the lights go out in his eyes as he slumped to the floor.

She threw the fire extinguisher aside, where it bounced with a loud thud. The sirens and alarms were still blaring, but she barely noticed them. Huffing and puffing for air, she gave him a kick in the vest with a toe.

"What do you think of Hawaiians now?"

Getting no response, she took the gun off his vest clip. Working with it, she tried to imitate what she saw Jeff do with his once, of taking out the small magazine. When it finally released, it fell to the floor and she kicked it down the hall. Wondering what to do with the gun, she held it out, the muzzle pointed to one side. He finger slipped to the trigger, and with barely any pressure, it fired one bullet.

"Wow, that was easy. I thought this thing was unloaded?"

Squeezing the trigger again, nothing happened. Hoping it was now safe to be left alone, she wondered what to do with it. That's when Jeff limped up to her. The kids had followed him. They all looked down at the man out cold on the floor, covered with white powder.

"Nice," he said with a note of admiration.

"What do I do with this?" she asked of the gun. "I don't want it falling into the wrong hands."

"Put it in a place where no one will look for it."

With alarms blaring, she made a hasty decision. Going to the kitchen, she put it in the refrigerator.

"Good thinking," Jeff said when Maile returned to the group. She took the blindfold bandana from around her neck and used it to tie the unconscious gunman's wrists together.

"You just go shut off the lights before anybody comes back. Somebody will have heard that shot."

Maile and the kids watched as Jeff limped down the hall to the janitor's closet. With one last nod from him, he went in. A moment later, sets of lights went off throughout the palace, the lowest floor turning dark last. For whatever reason, the alarms continued to blare.

"Holy cow, it's dark in here."

Malice at the Palace

Chapter Eleven

Maile walked with shortened steps, her arms extended in front of her. "Can anybody see anything?"

"I'm not sure my eyes are open," Bongo said.

Maile found the wall with one hand and tried to hurry using that as a guide. "Just go to the left until you bump into the wall, then follow that to the stairs. They're around here somewhere."

"Miss Spencer, can we hold hands?" Irene asked.

"That's a good idea. You guys should hold hands to make sure no one gets left behind. In fact, pair off into buddies."

"Like snorkeling?" Margo asked. "We learned about that yesterday in a snorkel lesson at Waikiki."

"Just like that. Stick together so nobody gets lost."

"There's nine of us."

Maile wanted to appoint Margo as mother hen to watch over the others, but didn't have time right then. "Somebody will have to hold my hand so I don't get lost."

Instantly, Maile felt a hand groping her until it found her hand. She squeezed it back while pulling it along. Maile tripped and fell when her toe found the stairs to go up. Righting herself, she found her buddy's hand and pulled it upstairs with her.

"Whose hand am I holding?" she whispered.

"Me, Miss Spencer."

"Okay, not to be existential, but who is me?"

"Evie."

"You and Evie are BFFs, Miss Spencer," Margo said.

"Won't ever get rid of her," Benny said.

"Shh! Quiet, Benny," Margo implored.

"I can't think of anyone else I'd rather have as a friend right now," Maile whispered as they got to the top of the stairs.

"Thank you, Miss Spencer."

When the group got to the landing, she did a head count. "Guys, is there any way you can call me Maile?"

"No, Miss Spencer. It's a rule at our school that we have to…"

Maile interrupted Margo. "Yes, your rule."

"Miss Spencer, who got shot?" Irene asked.

"Yeah, was the man on the floor back there dead?" Bongo asked.

"Nobody's dead. He hit his head on something and got knocked out."

"Why did he have that white stuff all over him?" Irene asked.

They still didn't have much light, but at least it wasn't pitch black as they went down the hall single-file.

"That was from the fire extinguisher." Maile wondered if she was lying to the kids with her explanation. "I asked him how to use it and he showed me."

"You clobbered him, huh?" the other Hacky Sack Kid asked.

"Maybe a little. But right now, we need to find our way to the Throne Room." She led them forward, still hugging the wall. When they got to the Throne Room, the kids followed Maile in. "Okay, this is where we have

Malice at the Palace

to be super quiet. No talking okay? We don't want the men hearing us." They all nodded in agreement. That had to be good enough. She knelt down to try to see Evie's face. "Are you still feeling okay?"

"My blood sugar is okay. Maybe I should've eaten a little more? I'm hungry again."

Maile had kept a stale dinner roll in a pocket from the kitchen just in case, and handed it over. "Just keep nibbling on this. I have your insulin and a syringe also, if you need it."

"Not the monitor?"

"I don't have many pockets. I just took what I could. But right now, you need to hold someone else's hand because I have a lot of stuff to do. Who's your best friend in the group?"

"I am," Irene said, coming forward. In the dark, it looked like they took hands.

"Okay, Margo, that makes you mother hen," Maile whispered. "You need to be in the back and make sure nobody wanders off."

"Yes, Miss Spencer."

Trying her best not to be too annoyed by the girl's officious voice, Maile went to the dais where the thrones were positioned and tried the door. As near as she could remember, she'd never been on the dais before. When she found the door locked, she cursed silently. She felt the door, the knob, and the gap with fingertips.

"Wait." She went back to the kids. "Dumb question. Anybody have a piece of wire?"

"Benny has fishing line," Margo offered. "He always has some."

One of the smaller boys dug through his pockets until he produced a handful of junk, all the usual paraphernalia that boys might have in pockets. He had a broken pencil, rubber bands, a crumpled flower pedal, a test tube with an insect corked inside, and a fishing lure with line attached. He untied the line and handed it over to Maile.

"Planning on going fishing later, Benny?" she whispered in the dark.

That's when running footsteps and excited male voices came from the hallway outside. As fast and as quietly as she could, Maile had the kids hide behind the partition behind the thrones. There wasn't enough space for her, so she crouched down to hide behind a throne. When the men came into the large room, two flashlight beams swept the floor and walls. Their beams paused on a spot across the room. While they discussed something in Arabic, Maile peeked at what they were looking at. It was a queen's formal gown on a mannequin on display. It was something the girls had wowed over earlier on the tour while boys looked at the thrones. Right then, in the dark room and flickering shadows made by flashlight beams, it almost looked as though Queen Lili'uokalani was standing there in her regal gown. After several more sweeps of their flashlights, the men started on a circular path through the room, flashing their lights around. It wouldn't be long before Maile and the kids were found.

Maile remembered the hacky sack toy in her pocket. Waiting for when both men were facing away, she threw the footbag toward the door. It flew through and bounced along the floor in the hall. That caught the attention of the men and they dashed out in search of the noise.

Maile mimicked for the kids to stay where they were. Going back to the door, she passed the fishing line through the gap between the doorjamb and the door. It took several tries before she was able to snake it around the simple door latch. Giving it a tug, the latch gave way and the door eased open.

"Somebody's watching out for us," she whispered.

Getting the kids again, they all crowded into the tiny room behind the throne dais partition. Closing the door instantly made it black inside.

"How'd you know to do that, Miss Spencer?" Margo asked. "With the fishing line?"

"My old door locks are the same at home. When I locked myself out once, a neighbor showed me how easy it was to pick that type of lock. Now I have more locks." She thought of the absurdity of the moment, that it had been Jeff Bedford, the head gunman and spokesman for Prince Aziz, that had been the handyman who'd installed her new locks. "Okay, on the floor in here is supposed to be a trap door to a tunnel. We need to find that trap door."

"Barely enough room for us to stand," Bongo said. "How are we supposed to look at the floor if we can't see it?"

Maile heard a swat of some sort.

"Bongo, quiet!" Irene said. "Do as she says and look for something. Maybe you'll find your brain!"

Maile was getting the idea some of them were brothers and sisters, and Bongo and Irene reminded her of she and her brother when they were kids. "You guys have been doing great. I'd appreciate it if you continued to get along for a few more minutes."

"You sound like a school teacher, Miss Spencer," Margo said.

"Yeah, why don't you scream at us?"

"As much as I'd like to right now, screaming wouldn't accomplish much."

The rug got shoved aside, and after a couple more minutes, Margo whispered, "I think I found a handle or latch."

"Where is it?" Maile asked.

"I'm standing on it."

"Can you move?"

"Only if I want to get friendly with Hennie, and she's not my type."

"You don't have a type, Margo," one of the boys whispered.

"Can we keep this serious, please," Maile whispered as authoritatively as possible.

There was panting for air as the kids crowded together at one side of the room no bigger than a bedroom closet. Maile hoped she didn't have another lock to pick as she felt the floor with both hands. Finding something that felt like a recessed handle, she gave it a yank.

It didn't budge.

She gave it another try, and a third, and fourth before giving up.

"Anybody know anything about trap doors?"

"Yeah. You can't open it if you're standing on it," Hacky Sack Kid said.

"Oh." Maile felt around again and discovered she was indeed standing in the middle of the trap. Stepping off, she gave the handle a powerful yank. There was some scraping, but the wooden door lifted free from the floor. Damp, stale air rose from the lower level, cooling the humid space they were in. Maile got out the flip phone and shone the screen light down inside the hole. Cobwebs stretched across in several directions. Using her finger, she broke those loose and reached further down. All she could see was an old wooden ladder built into one side.

"See anything?" someone asked.

"More cobwebs."

"Send Benny down there. He likes stuff like that," Margo said.

"I better go," Maile said. It wasn't easy letting go of the hand that was squeezing hers so hard.

Taking a couple of deep breaths to get up her courage, Maile put one foot on a ladder rung, following that with another foot on the next rung down. She wasn't sure if it was nerves playing tricks on her mind, or if a breeze was coming from somewhere filling her skirt with cool air.

After several rungs down, her foot touched down on what felt like solid ground. Stepping her other foot down, she let go of the ladder and felt the floor. It was hard, cool to touch, and damp. Feeling her fingertips, they weren't dirty as though she were standing on dirt. Using the phone screen light again, she shone it around her. Directly behind her was another door.

"Oh, great."

This door wasn't a simple wooden door, but iron. It was mounted on huge hinges that were bolted to an iron frame. There was no knob, but a wheel that needed to be turned. It looked like something she'd expect to find on a submarine, but heavily rusted.

Maile shone the phone light up the ladder. Nine faces were looking down at her. "Who's the strongest?"

"I am," Bongo said.

Someone snickered.

"I am, Miss Spencer," Margo said. "Want me to come down?"

"Please."

Once Maile was joined by the teenager that was as big as her, Maile explained what they needed to do.

"We need to turn that wheel to unlock the door, just like in a submarine. You hold that side of the wheel, and I'll hold this side. On the count of three, turn with all your might, Margo."

They both grunted and groaned for almost a minute before giving up.

"It almost felt like it was going to turn, but then it just seemed to push against me," Margo said.

"Which way were you pushing?" Maile asked.

"Clockwise."

"Okay, let's try again. Only this time we'll both push in the same direction, and that's counterclockwise."

"Backwards?"

"Right."

This time, the iron wheel budged, slowly turning. The problem was that it made loud grinding noises that echoed in the tunnel. Maile had the kids above them close the hatch before opening the iron door the rest of the way.

"Why do they have such a heavy door, Miss Spencer?"

"I think to keep people from sneaking in." Once they had the door open, they called for a couple more kids to come down. Irene was the next to arrive, with Evie right behind her.

"Who's going first?" Irene asked, trying to peer into the darkness ahead of her in the tunnel.

"I guess you, Evie, and I will go see what there is. You're not afraid?"

"No. Why should we be?" Irene asked.

"I don't know." Maile rubbed the chicken skin on her arms. "I sure am."

"I have to go in there?" Evie asked quietly.

"You need to be the first one that gets out of here and someplace where they can check your blood sugar. How are you feeling?"

"I think someone's behind me," Evie said.

"Those are the other kids." Maile got a cold shiver as a puff of wind went through. "I mean how are you feeling physically?"

"Gonna splash me shoes pretty soon."

"Huh?"

"She needs the dunny," Irene said.

"Okay, seriously..."

"Use the toilet."

"So do I," Maile said. "Just hold on for a few more minutes until we're out of here."

There was a groan ahead of them, a similar sound to the iron door they'd opened moments before. At least that's what Maile told herself. She wasn't convinced.

Maile led the way, holding the phone in front of her, breaking up cobwebs, holding Irene's hand, in turn holding Evie's hand as she followed.

"How long is this tunnel?" Irene asked after a moment.

"I hope only a hundred feet or so. Do you remember the Coronation Pavilion we looked at? The tunnel is supposed to lead there."

Maile tried figuring the direction they were heading by thinking of their route up to that point. Try as she might, she couldn't quite think of the exact direction, only that they were headed generally toward the ocean. After a couple of more minutes, they got to another iron door, similar to the first. This one was hanging ajar, though, giving her the idea it was what made the groaning noise earlier.

"That doesn't make sense. Nobody's in here ahead of us," she said more to the door than to the kids. "Margo, where are you?"

"Back here, Miss Spencer. I'm making sure we're all here."

"Good, thanks." That didn't explain why the iron door might've opened by itself. The occasional breeze that went through the tunnel was barely strong enough to close a bedroom door, let alone a rusty iron hatch. It took all of Maile's strength to push it halfway open. Once she had a big enough gap, she turned on the phone and shone the light through the doorway. "What in the world is that?"

"That doesn't look like the underside of a pavilion, Miss Spencer," Evie mewed.

"Sure doesn't."

"Doesn't smell like it, either," Irene said, pinching her nose with her fingers.

"I think this is the storm drain system."

"That would be better than what I think it is," Evie said.

There was a rumbling overhead.

"What was that?" the girl asked.

"Sounded like a truck. We're right underneath a street. I just wish I knew which one."

"Miss Spencer?" Margo asked in the dark.

"Yes?"

"Some of us have to use the loo."

"The closest one is back at the Palace, where the police are chasing the gunmen around the palace."

"I can wait."

"So can I."

"Me, too."

"I can't," Evie said.

"Me neither," added Irene.

"Okay, time for a potty break," Maile said. "Spread out and try not to go on each other's shoes."

After their break, Maile herded the kids through the iron door and pushed that closed. With the batteries growing weak in the cell phone again, she only flashed it from time to time to see her way forward. There was a trickle of water on the broken concrete floor now, easily side-stepped. The noise of the occasional vehicle overhead grew louder, and she felt the vibration of their rumbling. She heard a siren wail for a moment. Water dripped occasionally, catching her scalp and shoulders. She swiped away a drop of something from her cheek. Taking a few more tentative steps with her hands extended in front of her, something brushed against her face.

"Ugh. What was that?"

Maile swept her hand through the air and found what felt like a root hanging from above. Giving it a yank caused a miniature flood of water to splash down.

"Yeah, another great idea, Maile," she mumbled to herself. "Take your tour group through a tunnel in the middle of the night while being chased by maniac gunmen. This can be a part of the deluxe tour."

"Miss Spencer, it's getting mucky in here," Irene moaned.

"What's that mean?"

"You guys call it icky. Are we almost there yet?"

"I hope so. This is way more than mucky."

Maile felt a hand clasp hers, and she was glad to have one to hold right then.

They got to an intersection in the tunnel, with one way to the left, the other angling off to the right. A decision needed to be made, but at least there was no door to force open. It really was a simple coin flip decision, if she had a coin. Or light to see it. The last time she used the phone, the screen had gone dark, leaving the group in a cool, drippy place that had more puzzles—and puddles—than answers.

The hand holding hers seemed to pull to one direction. When she heard a vehicle go by, it sounded like it was coming in through a window.

"Which way did that come from?" Maile asked, training her hearing on both directions at once.

"Down here," Bongo said. His voice echoed off the walls.

When the hand holding hers tugged again, Maile took a couple of tentative steps. "Where are you?"

"Down here!"

"Please don't shout." Maile couldn't pinpoint the direction the echoes came from. "Where's here?"

"To the left."

"Does it go somewhere?"

"I think so."

With that, Maile heard hurried footsteps splashing through water. Still holding someone's hand, she led the other kids into the left tunnel. It wasn't any bigger, but had more water to walk through, a steady stream. After a few more steps, she felt a breeze on her face.

"I found something!" Bongo shouted.

When Maile and the others joined him, they looked out a long, narrow slot in a wall at eye level. There wasn't much to see, but at least it was of the outside world. A car going by in the street confirmed it.

"Where are we, Miss Spencer?" Margo asked.

Maile smiled at the image she saw across the street. "Not under the Coronation Pavilion, but someplace just as good."

Chapter Twelve

Maile gave someone's hand one last reassuring squeeze before letting go. There was a steel rod than spanned the length of the storm drain that came from King Street. Even if that hadn't been there, the gap would've been too small for any of them to squeeze through. She tried pulling on the bar anyway, the way a desperate prisoner would in his cell before execution. She looked across the street again to see the silhouette of King Kamehameha, his arm outstretched, leis hanging from it.

"The good news is that we're finishing our tour right back where we started it, at Kamehameha's statue. Just a little later than I planned. All we have to do is find a way out of here and up to the sidewalk." She slipped the flip phone from her pocket, hoping the battery had somehow magically come to life. It didn't.

"May I take a picture?" one of the boys asked.

"The phone's battery is dead."

"My camera should still work."

"We're not going back to the palace for your camera. Crazy men with guns, remember?"

"Got it in me pocket."

Getting it, Maile pried open the camera and popped out the battery with a fingernail, and did the same with the phone.

"Different sizes."

She gave back both devices to their owners to reassemble. Peering out across the street to watch Kamehameha stoically look back at her, she wondered

Malice at the Palace

how to attract the attention of someone in the middle of the night. All she could think to do was say a prayer.

"Who are you praying to, Miss Spencer?" Irene asked.

"Anyone that might be listening at this time of night."

"Want me to pray, too?"

"If you'd like."

When she heard Irene and a couple of the others muttering prayers, Maile continued to watch out the gap for activity. As the prayers ended, some singing started.

"Who's that?" Margo asked.

"Someone on the sidewalk!" All Maile could hear was the drunken lyrics of a man on the sidewalk above them. Unable to see him, she shouted anyway.

"Hey, brah! We need your help!"

The singing stopped. "Who dat?"

"It's me. I'm down here," Maile shouted.

"Down here where?"

"In the storm drain under the sidewalk." She used the camera to take a picture, hoping he'd see the flash of light.

Maile heard the squeaking of wheels as something rolled along the sidewalk. When that stopped, she saw two feet clad in old rubber slippers step down to the street level. A moment later, the broad face of a middle-aged Polynesian man with bushy hair looked at her. "Who you? The devil?"

Maile tried not to laugh. "No, Sir. My name's Maile. My friends and I are stuck down here and can't get out. Do you happen to see any police cars up there?"

"Whatchu need the police for?"

"To get out of here."

"Police for getting out of trouble. You need the sewer man to get out of the sewer."

"You're right." Maile was picking up the scent of booze on him, and the vibe that the man was homeless. If he was the man she often saw during her late-night runs through the city, the squeaking she'd heard would've been his shopping cart full of plastic bottles. "You wouldn't happen to have a cell phone, would you?"

"Try call sewer man? Triple overtime for working at night."

Rain was starting, and the streetside gutter was soon channeling water toward the drain. A small waterfall started, forcing the kids back.

"Do you have a phone I can use or not?"

"Gonna call the cops?"

"I promise I won't."

"Don't wanna go back to jail."

"You're not going back to jail. In fact, you might get a reward for helping me."

"Real thing? Cash money?"

Maile was using a hand to keep the rainwater from splashing her in the face. "Really need to use your phone!"

"No need for so much anxiety." The man went back to his shopping cart. Maile listened as empty plastic bottles were tossed out of his cart, bouncing around on the sidewalk. He handed over a smart phone when he returned to the drain. "Just charged the battery today. Don't get it wet."

Malice at the Palace

The phone was nice, especially for someone she figured was homeless. Tapping in a phone number she'd learned by heart, she waited. After it rang several times, she tried again. When it still wasn't answered, she sent a text.

Maile. I need help.

The phone rang a moment later. "Where are you?" Lopaka asked.

"In a storm drain on King Street, right in front of the Palace."

"What do you want me to do?"

"Call Ota. Maybe he can send someone to open a manhole cover."

"Ota's busy. He and the SWAT team raided the palace a few minutes ago. Maybe I can do something?"

"You're not at home?" she asked.

"I came back here after the Manoa House."

"Brah! Should've gone home."

"Not leaving you behind, Mai. Are the kids with you?"

"Yeah. They're getting the underground creepy tour of central Honolulu."

"Let me bring the van around and see what I can do."

Maile gave the phone back to the man and thanked him.

"What about my reward?"

"Oh, yeah. Can you wait a few minutes for the sewer man to get here?"

The man took up singing his off-tune song while loading bottles in his cart again. A few minutes later, she saw Lopaka park the tour van near Kamehameha's statue and scan the area. She used the camera's flash to signal her position.

Lopaka had a look of concern on his face, at least until they made eye contact. That's when he started to laugh. "Sistah, you're the worst tour guide ever."

"You the sewer man?" the homeless man asked Lopaka.

"Sewer man?"

"I told him he'd get a reward from the sewer man for letting me use his phone."

Maile watched as Lopaka got a few bills from his wallet. "You have a phone?"

"Nice one," the man said.

Lopaka stepped up to the sidewalk and Maile listened as they compared phones. "Hey! There's a lady and nine tourists stuck in the storm drain!"

The two men said goodbye and the squeaking wheels started up as the homeless man went down the sidewalk, once again singing. Lopaka went out to the street in search of a manhole cover. A moment later, he came back with a flashlight for her to use. "There's a plate at the corner. Maybe I can use a tire pry bar to lift it."

"Maybe we should call someone?" Maile asked.

"Who's responsible for manhole covers? It could take all night to find someone. Why didn't you call the police?"

"I promised that guy I wouldn't."

"You're too honest, Mai. Gotta get over that."

Maile watched as Lopaka moved the van to the curb at the corner to block traffic while he worked. She heard clanking and groaning, even some swearing. After a few minutes, Lopaka came back. "Too heavy for me. They make those things thick."

"There's no one around to help?"

"I'll get that homeless guy. He was big."

"Hey," she called out, catching him before he left. "Are there news reporters out there? I'd really rather not have this little escapade on TV."

"They're all on the other side of the palace where Ota set up a command and media center."

"Good. Do me a favor and flash a light down the manhole once it's open. We can't see anything down here."

It took a few more minutes before Lopaka and Shopping Cart Man pried up the man hole cover at the corner. A light was flashed, leading Maile and the kids to where Lopaka and Shopping Cart Man were waiting. Maile climbed the metal rung ladder first to make sure the way was clear. After swinging a hand around in a few circles to break up spider webs, she went back down to send the kids up.

"Evie, you're first. When you go up, make sure you stand on the sidewalk, and not out in the street."

Once Evie had climbed out, Maile sent the rest of them up the ladder of metal rungs set in concrete. She counted nine that went up, but shone the light in both directions to check for anyone else. Seeing she was the last one down there, she said a silent prayer of thanks.

Maile climbed to freedom. She checked the kids over on the sidewalk as Lopaka and the man shoved the iron manhole cover back in place with a clang as it settled. She used a bottle of water to wash their hands, and hankies to wipe faces.

"Okay, everybody on the bus," she said. She opened the cooler and food basket, and both were cleaned out. She sat with Evie to make sure she nibbled at the crackers she'd grabbed.

"Where are you taking us now?" Margo asked, eating cheese puffs from a bag.

"At three o'clock in the morning, your parents must be freaking out. Any idea where they are?" she asked Lopaka.

"I heard on the news they were assembled at the media center behind the Palace."

Maile eased her head back against the headrest, not caring where they went. "Media center it is."

***

Once the kids and their parents were reunited, Evie was checked over by paramedics. She continued to eat crackers as her blood sugar was checked and her diabetic needs discussed with her mother. The other kids gave explanations and told tales, while Maile was quizzed by police. Through it all, Maile had been able to sidestep news reporters. As Maile used handiwipes from the paramedics to clean her face and hands, Evie's mother found her. It would be the first explanation she'd have to give to parents in person, something she was dreading. Especially with Evie, who had held up remarkably well during their ordeal.

"Miss Spencer, may we chat a moment?"

"Yes, please. Let me explain a few things…"

"No need to explain anything. Evie has already told us about what you did for her and the others."

Malice at the Palace

"I really should've monitored her better than I did, but I never knew until later in the evening that she needs insulin."

"That's the remarkable thing, that you were able to find insulin for her. You must understand how grateful we are, for watching over her and the other kids like that."

Maile noticed one of the kids giving an interview to a news reporter. "You know what? It was Margo that was the mother hen. She's the one that kept everything under control."

When Evie's mother went off to talk with Margo's family, Maile went to check on Evie. She put on her biggest smile and hoped it looked sincere.

"Hey, look at you! Two big, strong paramedics and a police officer all watching over you."

"Hi, Maile," the girl said, nibbling away at a cracker.

"We just checked her blood sugar. A little low but still normal."

Maile listened as Evie told the story of having her blood sugar checked by a monitor that was smuggled into the building, making the whole thing sound a lot more daring than what it had been.

"Miss Spencer, is it okay if I write a story about this for school?"

"I think that's a great idea. I hope you send it to me to read."

"May I include the ghost? Would she mind?"

"Ghost?"

"My daughter has a vivid imagination when it comes to ghosts," the father said. "She could write a

135

report about potato farms and somehow a ghost will find its way in."

"This one was real, Daddy."

"When was there a ghost?" Maile asked.

"She's been following us ever since the lights went off."

It was a balmy night, but Maile got a shiver. "What did she look like?"

"Just like Queen Lili'wo…Lili'ka…darn."

"Queen Lili'uokalani?"

"Yes, just like her picture," Evie said.

Her father smiled at Maile. "See what I mean about her imagination?"

"Evie, you go ahead and include whatever you want in your story, and please send it to me. I'd like to hear about your ghost. She sounds very special to me."

Detective Ota found Maile as she was drinking some water given by a paramedic. He was grinning at her.

"Sure you don't want to work for the police department?"

"Being a tour guide is exciting enough." Somehow, it didn't feel finished. "Did you get all the bodyguards?"

"Got them. Already taken away."

It was a question she didn't want to ask. "How much shooting was there?"

"They gave themselves up with a single shot being fired. No tear gas, no blood, nothing."

"What happened with a docent named Mrs. Goodwin? I haven't seen her in a while."

"She came running from the back of the building about the time the lights went out. The paramedics had a hard time stopping her. She's pretty rattled, but okay. Got some good intel out of her about what was going on inside right then."

"What happened with Jeff?"

"The gunshot wound? Off to Honolulu Med. I did find one bullet hole in the wall, though."

"That was me. Don't ever hand me a gun. What about Aziz?"

Ota's face darkened. "He's still in there."

"Go get him!"

He took her away from the group that was forming around them. "Not so easy. Somehow, he got one of the guns. He's threatening suicide if we storm the King's bedroom. Plus, he has demands."

"I don't care about his stupid demands. I just don't want him to kill himself in the Palace. It's had enough trouble already."

"His demands concern you, Maile."

She watched as police cars took Australian families back to hotels in Waikiki. "I'm not marrying that jerk, understand? If he wants to put a bullet in his head because of that, I can live with it. But I'd appreciate it if it didn't happen in the King's bedroom or on palace grounds."

"That's not the demand. He only wants to leave the country, but he's taking you as a shield. He knows we won't try anything if you're with him."

"What's that mean?" she asked.

"We have a plan, and this one you won't interfere with. We need you to accompany him to the airport."

"Tonight?" Maile shook her head. "You have no idea how cranky I am right now."

"You don't have to negotiate anything with him. I doubt you'd even have to speak much. Just go in and tell him you're willing to leave with him."

Maile pointed her finger at the building. "You want me to go back in there? I just escaped from there!"

"He's the only one in there."

"And he has a gun," Maile said.

"It would be for only a few minutes before you left."

"Leave with him?" Maile asked.

"That's the idea, yes."

"Then what happens at the airport?"

"You might have to get on the plane with him."

"What? You just said…"

He waved her to calm down. "He's expecting you to go with him, and our negotiator has agreed to it."

"Maybe I'm not so agreeable! Did your negotiator think of that? Who in the world gave him the permission to make that decision about me?"

"I did." Ota took half a step back from her. "We're trying to plan a switch. But the only way Aziz is leaving that building without bloodshed is if you agree to go with him. None of us want that, Maile, and I think most of all you."

Maile looked off in the distance. A tall woman in a long dress was watching what was going on from inside the wrought iron fence that surrounded the palace grounds. As far as she knew, all the docents had been smart enough to flee at the very beginning, when Aziz and his guards moved in. Ota said the building had been cleared of everyone but Aziz, and the protestors went home when the dinner hour rolled around. No one should be inside the grounds at that point in time. Even at fifty yards away, it almost felt as if they were making eye contact when the woman nodded at her.

"Maile?" Ota asked.

"Yes?" Maile came back to the here and now of the moment. Looking back at the woman once again, she was gone. "Okay, what do you want me to do? I suppose I have to wear one of those wire listening devices I see in the movies?"

"We'll set you up with one in just a minute."

"What if he finds it?"

"He's probably expecting you to be wearing one." Ota called someone over, who happened to be someone she knew. "Turner, get her wired for sound, and put a vest on her."

After Ota went off to direct officers in cars, Brock smiled at her while holding the gadget in his hands, along with a bulletproof vest.

"I suppose you need to tape that to my bare skin?"

"On the center of your chest is usually best. I'll have to hide the end of it in the vest straps on the outside."

Maile hesitated, trying to think of a way out of wearing either the vest or the wire.

"Turner!" Ota shouted from where he was. "Time's wasting."

Brock pointed at Maile, ready to say something, but was interrupted by Ota.

"Spencer! Do as you're told, just this once!"

She looked Brock dead in the eyes. "I'm not taking off my blouse out here in public."

"It's dark and not many people are around. Otherwise, people see you in a swimsuit at the beach all the time."

She put her hands on her hips. "In my swimsuit, not in a bra."

"You can go in the ambulance and do that, if you like," one of the paramedics offered.

They both went in the back of the ambulance. Sitting on a small ledge, she removed her cotton blouse to let Brock position and tape the slender wires in place. His fingers were warm when he touched her skin. Every time he leaned close to apply more tape, she was embarrassed all over again.

"Sorry if I smell bad. Been a long day and I've been crawling through the storm drains."

"Not a problem." He handed her the vest to put on. "Straps in front. Make it as tight as possible."

"Why?"

"It works better at stopping bullets if it's tight."

She started working with the vest, figuring out how to put it on. "Brock, I've been mean to you lately."

"You have?"

"You haven't noticed?"

"I've been feeling some push back from you. I thought maybe…I don't know."

"I've been jealous. I know I have no right to be."

"Oh, you mean Mei-ling, Miss Wong, from the restaurant?"

"Yeah, and it's none of my business who you make friends with," she said.

Malice at the Palace

"She's none of my business anymore, either. Look, Maile. When you saw us at the waterfall that day, it was a part of an undercover investigation. That's all."

"Whose covers? Yours or hers?"

"Pretty nasty thing to say."

"And I'm pretty jealous. Nothing was going on?" Maile asked.

"Just undercover police work."

"That's what Ota told me, but I thought he was covering for you."

Once she had the vest cinched down as tight as she could and still take a breath, Brock positioned the tiny microphone behind a strap. He did a sound check with someone remote, and once they were satisfied it worked, she put her blouse back on over everything.

When he got up to leave the back of the ambulance, she grabbed him by the shirt and pulled back. For some reason, she was fighting tears. As crowded and clumsy as it was inside the paramedic ambulance, she drew Brock close and hugged him.

"What's this for?" he asked, putting his arms around her.

"I just want to know what it feels like." She pressed her face into his chest to blot an eye before pushing him back. "Just in case I don't come back in one piece."

"If the two of you are done, we still have a job to finish," Ota said from ground level looking in through the doorway at them.

Brock hopped down and hurried away, acting like he'd broken a rule.

"You okay?" Ota asked Maile as she hopped down.

"Great, now. That was my doing, not his, by the way."

"Finally one of you did something."

Maile had to change the subject. "How does this go again?"

"Just go in the back door and to the King's bedroom. After meeting him there, we'll allow his driver and car to come to the front entrance for the trip to the airport. This was all devised by him, and we've agreed, just to keep the whole thing peaceful. We'll have vehicles parked along the two or three common routes to the airport, along with a couple of cars following at a distance, to make sure there isn't some sort of alternate plan in the works."

"Like kidnapping me? You're allowing him to do that anyway."

Ota ignored her comment. "Just stick to the plan and everything will be fine."

"If he comes even close to touching me in that bedroom, I guarantee you there'll be bloodshed, and it won't be mine."

"Fine with me. Just don't get shot," Ota said.

"I suppose your SWAT team guys will have a sniper take a shot at him while we go to the car?"

"No snipers, no rush jobs. We're not risking a civilian life on this."

One of the FBI agents that had been listening came over. "I have snipers that will take a shot, if they have one. That's why you're wearing the vest, Miss Spencer."

"So, I'm leading a man to his gallows?"

Ota took the FBI agent away for a quick chat before returning to Maile.

"Forget that guy, and anything about a sniper taking a shot. You'll be fine, as long as you don't do something stupid."

"But you're sending me back in there," she muttered. "That seems pretty stupid to me."

"Half the point of the mike is so we can track what's going on with you at any given moment. All you have to do is keep up the chatter, letting us know where you are and what's going on. Also, try to remain facing him at all times and within a few feet, so the mike can pick up his voice better."

"That means I should say things like 'please don't shoot me' if he's aiming his gun at me?"

"That's the idea," Ota said.

"Please don't shoot me."

Ota chuckled. "You need something to eat? I think I can find a sandwich or doughnut?"

"I'm long past hungry. Let's just get this stupid airport plan started. I've always wanted to see Khashraq."

Chapter Thirteen

Once Maile was back in the building, she went to the restroom first. There she was able to wash more thoroughly, dab water on smudges of tunnel grime her clothing, and used a fingernail to clean her teeth. The little kitchen was her next stop. She looked in the refrigerator and found the hidden gun still there. Not as impressed with Ota and the FBI's plan as they were, she stalled for a few minutes to cook instant oatmeal, and even washed the dishes when she was done, just to put off the inevitable.

"Okay, it's time to go see a crazy prince with a gun that wants to take me home to meet his mommy."

She climbed the stairs as though she were going to the gallows. Arriving at the King's Bedroom, she knocked on the closed door.

"Yes?" an accented voice asked.

"It's me."

"Miss Spencer?"

Maile controlled her tongue. "Yes."

"Are you alone?"

"Yes."

"It's unlocked."

She let herself in, leaving the door open. When she saw the Prince standing in the middle of the room, she almost wretched.

"Put your dang clothes on!"

"Before I take you home with me, I want to know if…"

Maile aimed her finger at him as though it were a weapon. "If you want me to go anywhere with you, you had better put your clothes on, and I mean right doggone now!"

Arms folded across her chest, she watched as he put on a shirt, underwear, his long white robe, and his headdress. She didn't know what she had expected to see, but she wasn't impressed with him as marriage material.

The quilt on the bed was in disarray, but she forced herself not to want to straighten it. The gun he'd gotten from a guard was also there. He was closer to it than she was. Trying to get to it first was out of the question.

"You are wearing a vest," he said. "It is bulletproof, yes?"

"Yes."

"You must take it off before we leave."

"I'm not taking my clothes off in front of you!"

"You are afraid I will shoot you?"

Maile was sticking with the answer that was working so far. "Yes."

"I cannot shoot you. You will be the mother to my children."

"One of those statements is correct." She had two really good reasons not to take it off, one being a sniper was waiting for a chance to take a potshot at them in the dark, and she'd expose the wire microphone taped to her chest. "I'm not taking off this vest."

He got the gun and aimed it in her general direction. "Yes. You will."

It was time to send one last message to Ota and the FBI. "Okay, I'm taking off the vest now, only because you're aiming your gun at me."

Tired of the games, she hurried to unbutton her blouse. Once that was off, she yanked at the straps to remove the vest. That left the wired microphone, which she pulled free and tossed aside.

For as much running as she had been doing in preparation for the marathon in a few days, and with the weight she'd lost because of that, she knew her physique was still more feminine than his was masculine. As she buttoned her blouse again, she remembered Ota's instructions, to sell the idea that she really was going to Khashraq with him.

"You've seen my body. Will I be a good mother to our children?"

"We have wet nurses if you aren't."

"That's all I am to your family, a uterus?"

Aziz shook his head with confusion. "What is this?"

"A womb."

"You will accompany me on official events as a proper Arab wife."

"How can I do that? I'm Polynesian and Asian."

He walked in a circle around her, giving her a closer examination. "Plastic surgery for your face, more fat on your body, language for your voice, a new religion in your soul. Clothing and scarves will cover most of your body when in public." After the exam, he looked her closely in the eyes and smiled. "It can be done, even with someone like you."

He made a quick call in Arabic, and Maile assumed it was for his driver to bring the car. When he had her go

Malice at the Palace

first, Maile felt something touching he middle of her back, and hoped it was the gun.

It was a long walk down the stairs to the main entrance. It was already unlocked as though Ota and the FBI were expecting them to exit there. A large sedan was waiting out front, its engine idling.

Maile went down the steps. With each footstep, she expected to hear a shot, the Prince to fall, blood to splatter on her. She hoped the message got through, that she was no longer wearing the bulletproof vest, and that the sniper's shot was accurate.

When they got to the bottom of the steps, she still had another thirty feet to travel to the car. She took her steps carefully, one at a time, in a straight line. As much trouble as he'd been to her, and as disgusting as he was, she didn't want him slaughtered. But if someone was going to take the shot, she wanted it done.

The car had a glossy sheen to it, with droplets of mist beading together, running down the waxy paint in tiny rivulets. She saw her own face reflected in the tinted window as she reached for the door handle. Aziz's face was also there in the reflection. She closed her eyes as she released the door latch to open it, not wanting to see what might happen to the Prince.

Maile got in and scooted over to the far side of the back seat, with Aziz getting in after her. He closed the door. There was a brief exchange between him and the driver, before they left the driveway. She wasn't sure how she felt about the Prince still being alive.

She tried looking back to see if anyone was following. Not seeing any headlights behind them, and feeling a nudge in her ribs, she looked down to find the gun jabbing her.

"You must be happy to be going home," she said to the Prince.

"Yes, finally leaving this terrible place."

"America wouldn't be so terrible to you if you weren't so dishonest to it."

"I didn't mean America. I'm still looking forward to seeing more of it."

"Oh. Hawaii hasn't lived up to your expectations?" she asked.

"Pitiful place. That's nothing to be called a royal palace. Khashraq is a real kingdom with a proper palace. You'll enjoy life there."

Maile had to remind herself a gun was stuck in her ribs. "Have to get there first."

"Why should you not want to come to Khashraq?" he asked.

"I've lived here all my life. My family and friends are here. Honolulu is my home."

"Your family? I have met your mother, and that boy you call a brother. I've met your friends. None of them are anything like the people that will soon be your family."

The idea that he'd been close enough to her mother to have met her, disgusted Maile. It was another sacrifice, to remain calm and not let into him about it. "So, this is it? We just go? I'm not allowed to say goodbye to any of them?"

"You will soon forget all about them."

Malice at the Palace

That would be his biggest lie ever, that she could ever forget about her mother. Maile decided it was best to keep quiet.

When they got to the airport, a pair of security vehicles intercepted them. Instead of stopping the luxury sedan, they led it through a gate to a quiet area near the end of a terminal. When the sedan came to a stop, the prince had Maile get out, and again followed her. A private jet was there, the engines running, its retractable stairway down to the ground waiting for them. She felt a nudge to her back again, implying to keep moving.

Again, she waited for a gunshot to drop the Prince in his tracks.

"What about the driver of the car? Just leaving him behind?" she asked.

"I don't care about him. He's useless to me now that my need for him is done, just like those idiot bodyguards."

"How do you expect a woman to fall in love with you with that sort of mentality?" she asked as they got to the base of the steps. She looked around for anyone that looked like FBI agents ready to pounce on the Prince. As it was, the airport security guards were taking the driver of the sedan into custody, completely ignoring Maile and Aziz.

"I don't expect you to love me. I only expect you to produce an heir to the throne. That's what you have agreed to, yes?"

"Yes, and money."

"The quicker you produce a boy, and then a girl, the faster you'll be able to leave my kingdom, Miss Spencer.

But I think by then, you'll love the kingdom as much as you'll grow to love me."

She stopped midway up the steps and turned around to face him. The wind was steady, ruffling her clothes and tugging at her hair. "If I am to be your princess, then you will address me as such. My name to you for now on is Kamali'i-wahine Hokuhoku'ikalani."

"Yes, of course. Until you are provided a new name, one deemed acceptable to my Kingdom, not yours."

Even though the gun was pointed at the ground, Maile didn't take the swing at his face the way she wanted. Instead, she went into the cabin. She'd never been in a private aircraft before, and it was decorated much more elegantly than the ordinary airliners she'd been on. She barely noticed, though, because there still weren't any police or FBI agents onboard, only a female flight attendant wearing a head cover and modest clothing. The attendant hit a button, which brought up the steps to close the door. Maybe it was the gun that the Prince handed off to her, but the attendant seemed distracted.

"No one else is coming with us?" Maile asked.

"Only the pilots. Please, have a seat anywhere," the Prince offered. I shall be in my private compartment, sleeping. The attendant will bring you whatever you like."

"I'd like a ride home."

Aziz laughed as he went down the aisle. "You're very clever, Miss Spencer."

"Not clever enough this time."

Malice at the Palace

Maile stood in the middle of the aisle between single large seats on either side, watching as the Prince closed himself into a private room in the rear. She watched the steps come up and the door close. Going to a window, she looked out. No cars were rushing the plane, no armed police running toward them. She went to the other side of the plane and saw the same. She was locked in a plane with its engines running, the Prince in his suite, and an attendant forcing a pressured smile.

The attendant pointed politely to a seat. "Please, it's best if you have a seat."

Maile looked out the windows again, hoping to see police cars, security guards, anyone that might be headed for the plane. No one was coming to her rescue. Detective Ota had finally let her down, and at the worst time imaginable.

"But..."

"Please."

Maile plunked down into a seat, barely feeling the pressure of her body on the cushions. She ignored the seat belt, but took the cup of tea that was offered to her. She watched as the steam rose. The scent of it was strong and fresh. The jet sat still as the engines continued to run. The attendant closed curtains over the windows. No police were showing up outside. Nothing made sense.

As Maile lifted the cup to her lips, the door to the pilots' compartment opened. Out stepped a man in an aloha shirt and jacket. She saw past him at the other man seated in a pilot's chair. He smiled to her. She looked back at the first pilot again, to see him smiling.

"Huh?"

The man came down the aisle, smiling. "Miss Spencer, did you think I was going to abandon you?"

"Detective Ota?"

Brock followed Ota down the aisle past the attendant. They ignored each other as Ota and Brock went to the door to the Prince's private compartment. Rather than knocking, they opened the door and went in, closing the door behind them. There was the sound of scuffling and argument in two languages, before someone was slammed up against the door. After that was a whimper and sobbing. The door opened and the Prince was pushed out the door into the aisle, his hands cuffed behind his back. In the short time the Prince had been alone, he'd already disrobed to his boxer shorts. Seeing a near-naked bald headed skinny Prince like that would've been comical any other time, but Maile was still trying to figure out what was going on. She heard Aziz whimper as he walked past her, Ota following along behind. Everyone continued to ignore the attendant that was now standing at the control switch to activate the exit steps. Once the door was open, two men came up to put a new set of shackles on Aziz, followed by another man that went into the pilots' cockpit. In a moment, the engines began to slow, as Aziz was led down the steps to the tarmac.

Brock stopped next to Maile.

"Are you okay?" he asked.

"I don't understand. What's going on?"

"This was our plan all along. He needed to show true intent on leaving the island and American airspace before we could arrest him. Taking a hostage with him shows intent to traffic a person or persons against their will."

"He's going back to jail?"

"Permanently, this time. Stay here until he's clear of the airfield."

Brock joined Ota at the door and they went down together. Maile watched out her little window as men spoke and Aziz was loaded into a black four-wheel drive that had arrived, still only in his boxer shorts. Her biggest wish right then was that the scene could've been broadcast on network TV.

As the vehicle whisked away, Ota seemed to give the attendant the high-sign.

The attendant came back to Maile, now removing her scarf and veil. "I hate wearing those things," she said with a southern American accent. "You can go now."

"You're American? You work for the police?"

"Bureau agent. You sure looked worried, Ms. Spencer."

Maile stood. When her knees buckled, she sat again. After finishing the tea she'd been given earlier, she stood, hoping her legs would work. "I thought the next stop was Khashraq, with the obstetrician's office not far behind."

"Nobody was going anywhere, not with him."

"But the gun he had. He could've started shooting if he'd taken it to his little room."

The attendant got the weapon from its small storage compartment. She removed the small magazine. "Empty."

"How did you do that?" Maile asked.

"We didn't. The man we had there in the palace did. You met Agent Bedford, right?"

"Jeff's an FBI agent?"

"When we got word that Aziz was planning a takeover of some sort, and that his security detail was quietly asking for an English-speaking team leader to communicate with US officials, we planted him to control what was being done."

"But he's a handyman!"

"That was simply a way for you to meet him, Maile," Ota said, coming over to her when she got down to the tarmac. "We were hoping that if you saw someone you recognized, you'd be a little calmer during the Prince's arrest."

"That whole thing was a set up? Why didn't anyone tell me?"

"The less you knew ahead of time, the better it was going to work. But the Prince's security force was real, as was his takeover of the palace. That really threw us."

"Why'd you let me go in there?" Maile demanded.

The agent that had posed as the flight attendant excused herself, leaving Maile alone with Ota.

"You were going to be safe, as long as you went along with Bedford's plans and stuck close to him. And you did, right up until he was shot. That's when things started going off their rails."

"Yeah, people getting shot has a tendency to do that. What happened to all the bodyguards?"

"Taken in by the US Marshals. They're looking at lengthy stays in prison on numerous charges."

She watched as a police car arrived. "Now what? Am I going to be arrested for something? Or can I go home?"

"When was the last time you ate? You look like you need a meal."

"I had oatmeal at the palace a little while ago."

"You ate? So, that's what took so long."

"I can't survive on sewer gas, Detective." Maile clenched her teeth and emotions against the tears that wanted to fall. "Can I get a ride home? I need a long shower to wash the slime off me more than anything."

Chapter Fourteen

Just as Detective Ota had promised, Maile's name had been left out of the news reports about the temporary takeover of the Palace by Aziz and his gang of guards. The last thing she wanted was that sort of fame, because it often led to notoriety and a bad reputation. All the media got was that a guide from Manoa Tours was instrumental in capturing the 'squatting Prince' before he could leave the island. That's how the media ran with the story, that it was simply a deranged prince from a far off land that went a little nuts while on a private tour. While Manoa Tours would benefit from the exposure, what Maile didn't benefit from, however, was getting the secessionist protesters off her back.

Fortunately, she had no tours to give the next day, and planned to stay as far away from the Iolani Palace as she could. She still needed to take the bus past the place the next afternoon, and when passing by, she slouched in her seat and tilted her hat low over her eyes, just in case the spirits that inhabited the building were watching for her.

Her first errand of the day was to the law office of David Melendez, located in one of the few tall buildings along the Fort Street Mall, the modest downtown area of Honolulu. The office occupied an entire floor, and was decorated with etched glass privacy panels, potted plants, a large aquarium in the reception area, and soft sofas for waiting. Wearing a pleated skirt and simple blouse, Maile felt like a parochial school girl in the principal's office.

Malice at the Palace

The receptionist finished with one client before turning her attention on Maile with a smile. "Ms. Spencer, I can take you back to Mister Melendez's office."

"You know me?"

"Of course. We've been expecting you. Would you care for tea or coffee?"

"I'm fine, thank you."

When Maile was left alone, it was in a room with a large table, something that belonged in a boardroom. The receptionist had left the door open when she left. She still didn't have her phone back from Detective Ota, another errand for that day, so she had nothing to do to fill her time while she waited. After a moment, she wished she'd asked for the coffee that was offered.

There was a quick rap at the door and David came in, bringing two others with him. One was introduced as the office paralegal, the other being the law group's tax consultant. With a quick call to the receptionist, David asked for a pitcher of coffee and four cups.

"We drink a lot of coffee here, Maile. You may as well join us," David said. He put several forms in front of her, including legal papers, all of them with little red tabs indicating where she was supposed to sign.

"We really need to do this today? Honestly, I'm dead tired."

"I heard about what happened last night. Did you get some rest?" he asked.

"Yes, I'm just not as focused as I should be to sign legal forms. That's what got me in trouble the last time I did this."

"I'm not letting you sign anything that can come back to haunt you. It's also best to get this managed before the end of the year, just so taxes can be more easily managed. You've already mentioned that you might be leaving the island for a while after the first of the year. This is a lot easier for all of us if it's done in person."

She scooted the pile of forms to in front of her.

David started again. "Okay, a lot of things to go over today. If I go too fast, just tell me to relax. This first one is the official document that we'll send to Honolulu Med, acknowledging their settlement offer. As an ex-employee of the place, you know they don't have a parent company to deal with, making this process a lot easier for all of us. In fact, only one or two of the administrators are involved, with everything being dealt with through their legal department. None of your friends will ever know about this. Just sign where the red tabs indicate."

Maile spent a few minutes reading the document. Just as she was initialing and signing, the coffee was brought in and David poured for everybody.

"Okay, good. I still think we could get another million out of them, but it sounds like you're in a little bit of a hurry," David said. "Next, you need to pay taxes on that money, and that's a lot easier if you pay it right off the top and not have to deal with it later. I brought in our tax man, Reggie, unless you have someone you usually work with?"

"I've always done the forms myself. I've never had much other than simple income to deal with. I wouldn't know what to do with a tax man," she said.

Reggie took over. "These settlements are a little more complicated than simple income. I can set up a protected account until you know how you want to invest the money."

"Actually, I need to use some of that pretty soon. I'd rather just pay the taxes and put the rest in the bank."

"Reggie," David said. "No matter how hard you try, you won't be able to make Maile do something dishonest or illegal. I also know she has a few bills to pay, and probably would like to find a new place to live. A new set of wheels are probably in her near future."

Maile signed the tax forms that were presented to her by Reggie. The paralegal continued to sit and watch the proceedings, sipping coffee. "How do I get rid of an old car, anyway?"

"For yours, just call the auto junkyard and they'll send a tow truck. You might even get a few bucks out of the deal. I doubt a dealer would take it as a trade-in."

"Taking the bus is good enough for right now. What else do I have to sign?"

"Let's see. You agreed to the settlement, which includes back pay, and you've signed the relevant tax forms." David pushed everything to the paralegal to figure out what she needed to handle. "Looks like we're done sooner than I thought. Have you considered how to invest the money? Because simple savings will net you about thirty-nine cents a year."

Maile knew it was meant as a joke, but as tired as she was, she couldn't laugh. "How do I get the money? Is it a check?"

Reggie and the paralegal left the room, wishing Maile well.

"Not usually, unless you want it that way. Because of the taxes, there would be a wire transfer to one of our accounts, we'd deal with the taxes, and then transfer the remainder into whatever account or fund you decide on."

"Whatever is left after I pay your fees."

"That won't be much. There are legal filing fees that we'll make you responsible for, but we won't make you responsible for all the rest of this. You've already done plenty for me, and for Melanie and her kids."

"Look, David. That's very generous of you, and your cousin. I enjoyed having Therese here a while back, but I was generously paid by Melanie for that."

"That's not why we're providing pro bono services, Maile."

"I also know you have some personal interests…"

"Also not the reason why. with this hospital matter, I don't have to represent you in court, which would've been a huge time drain for me. That's where most legal fee hours come from, court prep and time. And as far as those personal interests go, I've put them on hold. I've heard that you have something going with a police officer, and I need to respect that. Anyway, at this point in time, you're a client."

"That's news to me. But why aren't you billing me for these services? You're spending a lot of time on me."

"That paralegal is managing most of this. Otherwise, you're one of the good guys in the world. You've had some rough knocks lately."

"Maybe. That doesn't mean I should get a free ride."

"Not a free ride. You still need to pay the fees, which won't be cheap. But billing you for time when the paralegal is managing most of it wouldn't make much of a difference in our firm. I know that sounds snobbish, but when we meet someone like you who conducts herself in a decent way and doesn't play the system for everything she can get..." David shrugged. "...I guess I feel a little soft-hearted about things like that."

Maile still wasn't sold. "I guess I'm one of those people who think of lawyers in a certain way because of their reputations."

"I imagine you know about my uncle, Melanie's father, being one of our presidents. She and her mother spent a couple of years living with him when she was a kid, and that's when we got to know each other. When they moved back to Maui, it was tough for both of us. We grew up treating each other more like brother and sister than cousins. But it's that President that links us together as family. I promise you, neither Melanie nor I are willing to risk his reputation by being greedy or insensitive."

"No romantic strings attached?"

"No strings attached. But when it comes time to invest that money, I'd appreciate having one of our investment gals on your list. And yes, they're honest."

"Thanks, I'll keep it in mind."

There was one last form that David gave her, a computer printout. "Here's this that you requested. I thought professional licensure was verified online these days?"

Maile read a website printout for RN licensees with her name on it. Piece by piece, her life was coming back into order. "Silly request, I guess. I don't have a printer at home and needed something for an official file. Thanks."

"Maybe you can wave that in the noses of HR managers when you go for interviews. I suppose you're already looking for a job?"

"My first interview is my next stop."

David closed the door. "There's something else, a legal matter that can't be handled by the paralegal, and something I need to talk to you about privately."

"Coming from a lawyer, it sounds like bad news."

"Maybe. It's about your ex-husband Robbie and his brother Thomas. He's your boss, right?"

"Yes, the owner of Manoa Tours, and now Robbie's old bar. Why are you bringing up that mess again?"

"It turns out that Thomas doesn't own the tour company."

"What?" As tired as her mind was right then, it began to spin. She'd handed over years' worth of wages to Robbie for the bar, and bought a van for the tour company. Now she was finding out it was going into someone else's pocket. "I'm gonna kill both of them. Then I'm going to…"

David patted her hand. "Relax. I checked on title ownership of the tour company. You're the owner of it, Maile."

"Me? I own Manoa Tours?"

"That's the way it looks."

"How can I be the owner? Robbie owned the tour company before selling it to Thomas, and then he bought the bar with the proceeds. Thomas has been running the tour company ever since. I had nothing to do with either one of those deals."

"Do you remember signing documents at the time of either deal?"

"We've already talked about this, David. There was paperwork that Robbie brought home. I made sure we weren't signing up for giant loans. Otherwise, I didn't look too closely."

"You should've. I received scans of the deeds and paperwork, and your signature is on the lines as owners of both places."

"Robbie used me?" Maile asked, feeling embarrassed.

"They both did."

"I'm so stupid. I shouldn't be allowed to have money."

"Apparently, neither of their credit was good enough to make either sale go through, and they both relied on your credit record. I'm still trying to figure out all the details of how the tour company changed hands and where the money came from that Robbie used to buy the bar."

"It came from me. I let him use the money from our savings to buy the place. The place was a dump, and that's why he got it so cheap. Then I gave him more money to redecorate the place. Then more money to keep it open when customers didn't flock in there. Then more, and more."

"How much altogether?" David asked.

"Deep into six figures over a period of the three years we were married." Maile shook her head. "I am such a sap."

"Actually, you're not. You wouldn't believe how often this sort of thing happens. In a way you were smart to figure out Robbie was dishonest and divorce him. Of the three of you, you're the only smart one."

"Does that mean his legal troubles aren't so bad? Because it wouldn't hurt my feelings at all if he spent a week or two in jail."

"That's up to the police and the District Attorney. But what I'm concerned about is the matter of the books being cooked. They've evaded paying some taxes these last couple of years, and you'd be responsible for paying those, and whatever fines were levied."

"And there goes the settlement?" she asked.

"The good thing is that neither business has been particularly profitable. Taxes are based of business net income, and the bar has probably shown a loss. Robbie only made it look like he was making money so he could sell it to his brother."

"But how could he sell it to Thomas if I own it?"

"Good question. Robbie's been pulling the wool over his brother's eyes, also."

"How does someone do that sort of thing? How does someone scam their own family?"

"I don't know, but you figured it out and Thomas didn't. Not many people would've seen through a scheme like that, at least not until it was too late."

"What do I do now? Wait for a tax audit?"

"Reggie, our tax guy, is already being proactive. He's working with the IRS and federal officials to sort through all of this. Yes, there will be an audit, but it won't be nearly as painful as what it looks like right now."

Being audited wasn't in Maile's plans for the coming weeks and months. "How long does that take?"

"Since we're being proactive, likely before the end of the year. That's why I'm in something of a hurry with this. We can have that here in the office."

"Home field advantage?" Maile asked.

"Exactly. Now you're thinking like a lawyer!"

David showed her to the door and bade her good luck. Shaking his hand, she felt like something was ending, maybe the chance at ever getting to know him better. She also wondered if there was something working behind the scenes. Even though she barely had a social life anymore, it seemed very complicated right then.

Leaving the building, Maile felt some pressure lift from her shoulders. She knew exactly how the money would be used, some going into the Manoa House fund, and the rest going into bank accounts. Maybe she'd even buy a long-term CD.

"Yeah, like I'm some kind of high finance expert."

Her next stop wasn't an appointment at all, but lasted an hour. She learned what she needed to know before going to the police station to meet Detective Ota. She was led to the squad room by a reception clerk where he had his desk.

"You need a leash for this thing," he said. He took her phone from his desk drawer and handed it over. "Get any sleep?"

The first thing she did was check for messages. "Some. I'm still a little wound up over what happened last night. Did the kids get back to their hotels okay?"

"Safe and secure with their parents. From what I heard, they're taking one day off from sightseeing before starting over again. By the way, there's a press conference in two hours. Some of the kids will be there with their parents. It'd be nice if you joined us."

"I'd rather not get the Spencer family name mixed up with something like this. It's not just me, but my brother and mom would have to live with it. Just mention the name of the tour company a couple of times, and that'll make Thomas happy." Maile considered the sudden revelation that she was in fact the owner of the tour company. "What's happening with Robbie?"

"The DA told me to cut him loose. From what I understand, he was never the owner of the bar to begin with. I asked who is, but the DA wouldn't give me a name. But they're looking into that person's activities. I think it's a shill, somebody using the place for tax evasion."

"Maybe so." Maile fidgeted in her seat, wondering if she should let him in on her secret about the bar ownership. "I don't want to ask but I need to know. What's going on with Aziz?"

"He's in federal lockup. Mrs. Abrams has a laundry list of charges to bring against him, and feels certain most of them will stick."

"And I'm her star witness again?"

"Probably. It's funny, though."

"I don't see anything humorous about that guy at all," she muttered.

"You'll like this. Mrs. Abrams was ready to cut the guy loose and let him go home, if he promised to never return to US soil. A few days from now, he could've walked onto his plane and flown off, a free man."

Maile chuckled, but without mirth. "Instead, he held a bunch of kids hostage, and acted like a dirty old man around me. And someone had to get shot because of it."

"Yes, Bedford. I checked on him this morning. He'll be okay, physically."

"I imagine he's going to prison for a while?" Maile asked.

"Funny thing about him."

"And again, I don't see much humor in what happened last night, Detective."

"He's a fed. He was a plant by the FBI."

"It's true what that woman agent told me this morning at the airport?" Maile asked. She'd completely forgotten about Jeff being an agent.

"Absolutely. I never knew it either until the problem at the Palace. When I checked him out a while back, all I found on him was that he'd been in the military, recently arrived from the mainland, and now worked as a handyman."

"But he said Aziz hired him to be his security advisor and spokesman."

"And that's also correct. Aziz wasn't very smart about that. Pretty naïve, in fact. He looked rather openly for someone to fill that position, and when the Bureau agents heard about it, they had him go in. The way I hear it is that the only way he got the job was because he was cheaper than the others, and there weren't many others. Aziz doesn't have much of a rep internationally, Maile."

"He's slime, living under a filthy rock."

"Which is his international rep," Ota said.

"What I can't figure out is why you and Brock were pretending to be pilots of Aziz's plane? Why weren't the

FBI doing that? That whole set-up yesterday to nab Aziz was a federal thing, wasn't it?" she asked.

"The FBI and the US Marshals had their hands full with the bodyguards, securing the building, and managing the next part of their plan of getting you and Aziz to the airport. Because of you going off on your own escape plan, major changes needed to be made."

Maile looked away. "Nobody died, and the kids got back to their parents, safe and sound. That's what matters to me."

"Bedford and the local Bureau office are recommending some sort of commendation for you."

"Does it pay the bills?" she asked.

"No, but it might be something to hang on the wall. Maybe a little ceremony to go with it."

"They can put it in the mail." Maile's mind was already turning over plans for the future, and Ota might be able to help with something. "What's new with your daughter, Suzie?"

"We never have discussed her, have we?"

Maile was sure to make eye contact. "No, we haven't."

"She was the light of my eye. Then she started junior high and fell in with a new crowd. That's when her mother got sick, which put all of us under more stress. When I paid more attention to my wife Louisa than I did to Susan, it seemed to give her permission to go a little wild. By the time Louisa passed, Susan was in high school, or at least should've been. It wasn't long after then that she…" He shook his head. "…took up residence in the cellblock. It turns out that I lost both my wife and daughter to cancer."

It was turning out that she was going to give the same lecture to Ota that David gave to her earlier.

"That happens to a lot of families, far more often than you realize. But the good thing is, you still have your daughter. Maybe you can start mending the bridge between the two of you?"

"I didn't know you were such an optimist, Maile."

She laughed for the first time all day. "I've become a fatalist, at least with my own life. But I have some ideas of how you can help her. Let me think about it for a while and I'll let you know. Then you can decide how much of a crackpot idea it is."

"Maybe a crackpot idea is what's needed for her?" Ota began shuffling papers on his desk, as though he was wrapping up their visit. "Honolulu Marathon next week, right?"

"Unless I can think of something else better to do that day. I have a question for you. Are you any good at home repairs?"

"The house is still standing. Why not just hire a handyman to help you?"

"After Bedford and Aziz, forget it. Is there trouble if I fix the hole in the wall I made at the palace yesterday?"

"That's right. Bedford said you had a shoot-out with a bare wall."

"I'm not sure who won. Will I upset the police department if I fix that hole?"

"The evidence team has already collected the slug and taken all their pictures. If there's no crime scene tape protecting the wall, do whatever you want to it. Don't they have someone that can do that?"

"I broke it. I need to fix it."

"Speaking of things that need to be fixed, what's new between you and Turner?"

Maile stood, ready to leave. "Good question."

He waved her to sit again. "It's a done deal to you? No matter what he might do, you're done with Turner?"

"I saw him kissing Miss Wong, from the restaurant."

"Oh? I hope he wasn't."

"Why?" Maile asked.

"Officers aren't supposed to do that sort of thing during sting operations of suspects."

"Suspects of what?" she asked. "Forget it. I don't want to know. All I know is that he and Miss Wong looked very chummy at the Manoa Waterfall a while back."

"I'll have to talk to him about that. But before you doom him to being an almost-ran in the Romance Handicap, you need to know something. HPD has been investigating Chop Suey City for several months."

"That's what he said. What for?"

"Money laundering. Our problem is that we don't know where the money comes from or where it goes to. All we know is that large amounts pass through its doors, far too much for a restaurant. Hopefully, and I'm keeping my fingers crossed that Turner hasn't crossed a line, that the investigation is still on track."

Maile was conflicted. She'd already assigned Brock to the romance dustbin, even in spite of the hug she'd given him a few hours before. Whenever she thought of him, she'd get images of him with Miss Wong stuck in her mind. Now, Ota was telling her about a different situation. Or maybe it was different. "Where do you get the idea that money is going through their doors? Your new jailhouse snitch, Lefty Louie?"

"What makes you think of Lefty Louie?"

"I don't know. Just a name."

"Once again, you've been rather prescient. We have an informant named Lu, spelled L-U, that has found a way into the organization. Lu just happens to be left-handed. Is there something you know that I don't?"

"Does no comment keep me out of a jail cell?"

Ota chuckled. "For the time being."

"Does that mean I can go? Because as tired as I am, I can't risk my mood getting any worse, and I still have my mother to deal with." She stood, ready to leave. "Next Sunday is the marathon. On Saturday, the Manoa House is having a potluck at the Ala Wai ball fields, near the canoe center. You're welcome to join us, if you happen to take a day off."

"I'm not a member."

"I'll make you an unofficial Hawaiian and member of the club for the day."

"I wouldn't have a date."

"Bring your daughter." Before leaving his desk, she had one last message. "Tell her to dress nicely. My friends will be there."

...

Malice at the Palace

More from Kay Hadashi

Maile Spencer Honolulu Tour Guide Mysteries
AWOL at Ala Moana
Baffled at the Beach
Coffee in the Canal
Dead on Diamond Head
Honey of a Hurricane
Keepers of the Kingdom
Malice at the Palace
Peril at the Potluck

The June Kato Intrigue Series
Kimono Suicide
Stalking Silk
Yakuza Lover
Deadly Contact
Orchids and Ice
Broken Protocol

The Island Breeze Series
Island Breeze
Honolulu Hostage
Maui Time
Big Island Business
Adrift
Molokai Madness
Ghost of a Chance

The Melanie Kato Adventure Series
Away
Faith
Risk
Quest
Mission
Secrets
Future
Kahuna
Directive
Nano

The Maui Mystery Series
A Wave of Murder
A Hole in One Murder
A Moonlit Murder
A Spa Full of Murder
A Down to Earth Murder
A Haunted Murder
A Plan for Murder
A Misfortunate Murder
A Quest for Murder
A Game of Murder

The Honolulu Thriller Series
Interisland Flight
Kama'aina Revenge
Tropical Revenge
Waikiki Threat
Rainforest Rescue

CPSIA information can be obtained
at www.ICGtesting.com
Printed in the USA
LVHW041927160621
690392LV00002B/365